# STALLIONS
## AT
# BURNT
# ROCK

WEST ★ TEXAS
SUNRISE

# STALLIONS
## AT
# BURNT
# ROCK

*A Novel*

# PAUL BAGDON

Fleming H. Revell
A Division of Baker Book House Co
Grand Rapids, Michigan 49516

Published by Fleming H. Revell
a division of Baker Book House Company
P.O. Box 6287, Grand Rapids, MI 49516-6287
www.bakerbooks.com

Printed in the United States of America

Library of Congress Cataloging-in-Publication Data

Bagdon, Paul.
    Stallions at Burnt Rock : a novel / Paul Bagdon.
        p.     cm.  —  (West Texas sunrise ; bk. 1)
    ISBN 0-8007-5798-X (pbk.)
    1. Women horse owners—Fiction. 2. Women ranchers—Fiction.
   3. Texas, West—Fiction. 4. Ranch life—Fiction.  I. Title.
PS3602.A39 S73 2003
813′ .54—dc21                               2002011454

To my favorite and most cherished
ladies in the world:
Sarah Bagdon and Tessa Kenney

# 1

Lee Morgan loved this time of day.

At dusk—shortly before sunset—the colors of the sky became more precise and clear for a few brief moments, and then a quiet peace took over. The colors became muted and soft, and even the air somehow became more gentle as the sun eased down.

Dixie, the old mare Lee was sitting on, dropped her head to crop grass. Lee scratched the horse's neck but didn't take her eyes from the Busted Thumb Horse Farm.

Her six hundred acres were a good mix for this part of West Texas. She had more grazing grass than useless scrub, a pond that lasted through the summer, a dependable sweet-water well near the house, and even a few widely scattered groups of trees.

Taking a step ahead, Dixie stumbled slightly, the evening light too dim for her seventeen-year-old eyes to discern a prairie dog hole. Lee intuitively shifted in her saddle to keep balance, a movement that was as unremarkable and as natural to her as breathing. When she'd jokingly say that she'd spent thirty-five of her thirty-nine years on horseback, she wasn't far from the truth. She rode better than most men, most cowhands, even most trainers and breeders. And that was a rare thing in Texas ten years after the War Between the States. Women didn't own ranches, nor did they spend their days in the saddle, directing men at their work.

Lee knew she was a bit of an oddity in Burnt Rock, the small town near her ranch. But she couldn't be bothered with that. At the rare times she gave the idea any thought at all, a grin would spread across her deeply tanned face.

The metallic clang of the "danger" bell snapped Lee and Dixie to attention. Lee swung the old horse back toward the ranch and urged her into a shambling lope— her fastest speed. But Dixie soon sensed the urgency of her rider and extended her stride until it almost approached a gallop.

*I shouldn't have left her side,* Lee thought as she approached the ranch. *I thought she had more time . . .*

Lee felt the eyes of the half dozen men clustered by a stall in the breeding/birthing barn follow her as she jumped off Dixie. Carlos, her long-time ranch manager and brother in Christ, stepped out from the others.

"She no doin' good. Much blood comes," he said.

Lee lightly touched his arm and then stepped around him as one of the men swung the stall door open for her.

The chestnut mare was on her side in a bed of clean straw that was rapidly turning dark around her hindquarters. Her body was sheathed in a patina of sweat, and her eyes were wide as she writhed helplessly, squealing at the pain she couldn't escape. Lee forced herself to stop, take a deep breath, and assess the situation, just as her uncle Noah had taught her to do many years ago.

Clover, a three-year-old, was one of Lee's favorites. She had all the qualities Lee looked for in a broodmare: strength, a wide chest, straight legs with good-sized, healthy hooves, intelligent eyes, and the endurance of a steam locomotive. Lee crouched next to the horse's head, cradling it, and whispered to her while gently rubbing the side of her neck. The mare's muscles were as hard and as rigid as lengths of cold steel, and every few seconds a spasmodic shiver ran through her body.

Lee, still crouched, still crooning softly, worked her way back to the mare's hindquarters and pushed her cloth-wrapped tail aside. Blood from the mare's womb ran brightly and steadily, glistening red under the sharp light of the lanterns.

Placing her hands on Clover's stomach, Lee pressed down, bringing another squeal of pain from the horse. The shape and position of the foal was apparent, even through the mare's trembling, sweat-soaked hide.

"Carlos," Lee said, struggling to keep her voice from wobbling, "get the sharpest gelding knife—and plenty of fresh water and clean cloths. Have one of the men clean a bucket and fill it with water and heat it until it's warm. Then I want you to add half a bottle of laudanum to it and mix it well. I need the funnel and hose too."

Clover squealed again, sounding almost like a woman as the next spasm took her. Lee took a deep breath. *Lord, help me with this fine horse you created.*

She slid her hand inside the mare. Warm blood gushed on her forearm and spilled out onto the soaked straw. Clover moved away from Lee's hand, but then was still as Lee's fingers found the foal's spine in the birth canal.

"Carlos!" she yelled. "The foal's spine is in the birth canal, not its head. Are you ready with the laudanum? Do it now—hold Clover's head up and dump it down her throat. We don't have time for the funnel or the hot water!"

Carlos clamped the fingers of his left hand on the pressure points on either side of the mare's jaw, forcing her mouth open. Clover's tongue lolled out limply, far more dry than it should have been, and she cried again in pain. Carlos lifted the bucket and began pouring a steady stream of the painkiller mixture into Clover's gaping mouth.

Lee watched as the liquid flowed down the animal's throat. She knew a horse has no gag reflex, no way to vomit. What could ease Clover's pain could also drown her.

When Carlos finished administering the painkiller, Lee forced her hand deeper into the mare, following the spine of the foal. The laudanum had worked rapidly—Lee felt the walls of Clover's uterus relax slightly. She breathed a sigh of relief, then probed deeper. "Please, Jesus . . ." she whispered.

She felt the foal's head. Then she felt the slippery velvet of an ear laid against the head. Grasping at it, she used all the strength in her hand, wrist, and forearm to tug the head into a delivery position within Clover's womb. She dragged the infant's muzzle down and forward . . .

The foal slid out of his mother perfectly, into Carlos's waiting hands. The ruptured cord, still pumping blood, no longer mattered. Carlos's knife flashed under the lanterns for a moment, and then mother and infant were separated. He tied the knot as capably and as quickly as he'd cut the cord.

Carlos looked at Lee. "We done good—all the blood come from Clover's cord an' her bag that hol' the baby." Just then, Clover's head swung back. Carlos grinned. "I thin' she looks for her baby," he said as he wiped the foal down and put him at the mare's side.

Lee nodded and stood wearily. She looked down at her hands and arms, which were gory with blood and afterbirth. Then, brushing away a few strands of sweat-soaked ebony hair from her face, she turned to the men gathered around the stall.

"Clover's fine now," she said. "And so is her baby—a colt, gentlemen—maybe our key stallion one day!"

As the men cheered and then wandered back to their bunks, Lee began wiping her hands and arms with a clean cloth. She gave up when she saw she was accomplishing little. *I'll just take a bath before I crawl into bed—no matter how long it takes to heat the water.*

She smiled as she turned to Carlos. "A long night," she said.

"*Sí.* But a good one."

"Maria will be back tomorrow morning?"

Carlos nodded. "I stay with Clover until she come. Then I go to town to watch thees bronc man with you."

Lee sighed. "If he's as good as we've heard, we've got to hire him. We have unbroken and untrained horses coming out of our ears, my friend."

"Ees true," Carlos agreed. "Tomas should no 'ave left as he did. One day he here—and then poof! He gone."

"I know. I know." Lee sighed again. "But that's over and done. We need to get a good man in here soon—we can't sell these horses as they are. And they're just get-

11

ting wilder out on the pasture, fighting, running mares, crashing fences . . . " Lee suddenly felt too tired to speak.

"I pray thees boy—thees man—whatever he ees—he be the one we need an' he come with us. You weel go to the celebration early tomorrow?"

"Yes. And I'll take the wagon—there's an order at the mercantile for us." Lee began walking toward her cabin, then turned around. "Greet Maria for me, Carlos. I'm sure she'll have a lot to talk about."

Carlos grinned. "She thin' the sun rises an' sets on thees baby. 'Our first grandchild,' she says, 'will be a great man, an' rich, an' own much good land as far as a fine horse can go in three days in all directions.'"

Lee returned the smile. "I'm sure he will."

Lee watched as the man stood motionless with one hand on the saddle horn, facing the trembling horse with the white cloth tied across its eyes. Around the small paddock in which the man and the horse were positioned, the Burnt Rock Fourth of July celebration filled the midday air with the sounds of laughter and excitement. Little girls screamed and shrieked as little boys chased them. Gunfire from the shooting competition cracked and boomed. Strings of popping, fizzling, and sparking Japanese firecrackers punctuated the air. And the strident shouts of barkers hawking their souvenirs, sarsaparilla, and small American flags tacked to wooden sticks were almost melodic in their repetition.

Lee wiped her hand across her forehead and pulled on her floppy sunbonnet to better shade her face. The huge white sun was flexing its summer muscles that day, but judging from all the noise, the men and women and children were doing their best to ignore the oppressive heat.

12

Lee tried to block out the noise and concentrate on the man and horse in the paddock. As she leaned forward on the plank seat of her farm wagon, her dress became twisted. She smiled bemusedly at the concession she'd made for the town today—she wore a long summer dress rather then the culottes she'd discovered in the Montgomery Ward catalog a couple of years ago. Allowing her to sit astride a horse comfortably and modestly, the French fashion was perfect for her. Of course, Lee knew that what was accepted as ladylike in West Texas differed a great deal from what went on in France, but she didn't spend much time worrying about such inconsequentials.

A meandering wisp of breeze toyed with her hair, ruffling her bonnet and cooling her face. She swiped perspiration from her forehead with the back of her hand without taking her eyes from the paddock. The horse, a deep bay stallion, was sheeted with sweat. His muscles were taut, rigid—looking as if they could burst through the skin that covered them. The man, talking to the animal so softly that Lee could only see his lips move, eased his left boot up toward the waiting stirrup. The motion was precise and smooth and unhurried—and yet in less than a heartbeat, he was in the saddle and reaching toward the fabric covering the animal's eyes.

Before the cloth touched the ground, the horse was in the air, launching himself upward, squealing and snorting toward the cloudless sky. He hit the ground clumsily, all four hooves slamming down at the same time, jolting the rider with the impact. Lee noticed that not a sliver of light was showing between the cowboy's seat and the saddle. She grinned. As the stallion leaped again, the man's boot heels thumped the horse's flanks. When Lee saw that those boots were spurless, her grin widened.

The rider's battered Stetson was long gone, snapped away by the raw power of the first jump, and his hair, the sun-bleached blond of a man who lives outdoors, flailed about his head with each move of the frantic bay. As the horse spun crazily, long strands of spittle from its gaping mouth whipped across the rider's chest and face. The stallion's hooves moved too fast for Lee's eyes to follow, and they spewed dust and grit into the air like a whirlwind.

But the rider sat tight, his face grim, his legs molded to the horse's heaving sides. Centered in the saddle, his body absorbed each twist and impact created by the animal underneath him.

Lee didn't notice that Carlos had joined her until he spoke.

"The Thumb need thees boy," he said.

"Yes, we do," Lee answered, her attention not wavering from the battle unfolding in the paddock. "Now he'll wait out the stud—if he can stick to him that long."

"He steek. No question."

Lee nodded. Carlos had been with her for eleven years, helping her run the growing horse operation that moved two years ago to the spread outside Burnt Rock. She and the Mexican vaquero had established a close and enduring relationship based on mutual respect, trust, and the love of fine horses. She firmly believed their friendship had made the Busted Thumb Horse Farm the success it was rapidly becoming.

As Lee thought about her ranch, she had to suppress a chuckle when she recalled how the operation had gotten its unusual name. Before all the fences were up, Carlos had been a bit careless tossing a loop over the neck of a skittish colt, and his right thumb had been broken when the youngster spooked and slammed the

14

man's hand against his saddle horn. A few days later, when Lee, Carlos, and Maria were discussing names for the new operation, Carlos would have no other than the Busted Thumb. "Ees a good, man-type name," he growled. "Ees men buy horses, not women. Ees good name." Neither Lee nor Maria could argue with that logic.

Lee turned her attention back to the horse and rider. The stallion's leaps were lower than they'd been a few minutes earlier, and he landed sloppily, almost falling several times. Over the sounds of the celebration, Lee could hear the eerie whistle of the exhausted animal dragging air into his oxygen-starved lungs. The rider's face was pale and streaked with dust, which stuck to the rivers of sweat that soaked him and turned his shirt to a sopping wet rag. But he sat tight and straight.

The horse whirled in a final attempt to dislodge the man on his back, leaping as high as his earliest attempts had taken him. When he came down, he struck the ground with such force that the rider's nostrils began seeping blood. Then the defeated stallion stood still, his head hanging as if in shame.

The rider hauled up the horse's head with the rope attached to the halter and used his heels to urge the animal into a stumble-footed couple of circuits around the small pen. He pulled his hand and forearm across the lower part of his face, leaving a red streak on his tanned skin and the worn fabric of his shirt. He pinched his nostrils closed as the stallion under him walked the circle once again.

"I'll talk with heem," Carlos said. "We can pay how much?"

"We'll find the money somewhere in the budget," Lee answered. "Don't let him get away."

She climbed down from the wagon, adjusting her bonnet with hands she hadn't realized were trembling, and made her way to the middle of the block that comprised the business section of Burnt Rock. Some of the men nodded to her, and several touched the brims of their hats. And although the women she knew smiled at her, she felt the sensation of being inspected and appraised by the townspeople—and not getting much approval.

Lee sighed audibly and then immediately hoped no one had heard her. She was the oddity, she knew, not the folks who observed her as if she were a two-headed calf. Women didn't own businesses, and they most certainly didn't own horse ranches where such activities as breeding and the castration of stallions took place.

But Lee simply shrugged this thought away and headed to O'Keefe's Café. Although there was only a few degrees difference between the inside of the small restaurant and the outdoors, the café was like an oasis in a scorching and airless desert. The almost blinding intensity of the sun stayed outside, making the dim light in the café at least *seem* cooler. And Bessie O'Keefe made the best lemonade in Texas. The beverage was expensive—eight cents per large mug—but lemons were hard to come by in West Texas, and the ice necessary to keep the drink cold was costly. It was a rule of the restaurant that anyone who complained about the price after drinking a mug of the lemonade got his or her money back. Neither Bessie nor her father, Mike, had ever been called upon to return a customer's eight cents.

Bessie, as ever, looked cool. Lee had seen her twenty-six-year-old friend handle the entire dining room on a busy afternoon, keep a steady stream of pies flowing from the oven, refill coffee cups, and take and deliver orders without a hint of moisture on her face.

"How do you do it, Bessie?" Lee said, greeting the young lady. "It's so hot out there the rattlesnakes are wearing hats, and you're as cool as can be."

"Mike doesn't allow me to perspire," Bessie said, louder than was necessary. "He says it slows me down and cuts into his profits."

A masculine "Hush, girl!" came from the kitchen where Mike was working. Most of the customers chuckled. Lee knew they'd heard variations of this banter many times before.

"Lemonade?" Bessie asked.

"I think I'm going to need two today, but let's start with one." Lee settled into one of the pair of wooden chairs at a small table and sighed deeply, grateful for the relief her feet were experiencing as she took the weight off her pinching, constricting high-button shoes. *Never again,* she thought. *I don't care what the occasion is. I'll either wear my boots or go barefoot.*

Bessie surveyed the other tables and then sat with Lee, placing a mug of lemonade in front of her. "Having a good time?" she asked.

After taking a long series of swallows, Lee answered, "It's a real nice celebration, Bessie. I heard the band earlier, listened to a speech, watched the buffalo hunters shoot. And I watched a young fellow ride a stallion into the ground."

"Men were gambling on that, you know," Bessie said. "I wouldn't have any part of it if I were you. Scripture warns us against gambling."

Lee drank again. "I wasn't gambling," she said. "You know that. I'm in the horse business, and I was interested in the rider. Since Tomas left we don't have a bronco man. We need one."

As if placated, Bessie leaned forward, closer to Lee, and lowered her voice. "He was in this morning for breakfast," she said. "He has the nicest manners a person could hope for, and the deepest blue eyes . . ."

"I'm sure he has," Lee said, grinning. "What's his name? Where's he from? All I've heard are rumors from my ranch hands."

"He told me his name's Wade, but he didn't give a last name. I was too busy to chat more than a few seconds. I heard from someone else that he worked breaking horses for the Confederacy and after the war went to some big outfit—Goodright? Good something or other, anyway."

Lee nodded her head. "That'd be Charlie Goodnight. He has the largest herds of cattle and horses in Texas. This Wade must be awfully good. Mr. Goodnight is cautious about who he signs on."

Bessie leaned forward again. "He isn't much older than I am. When he smiled at me—"

The opening of the door drew the attention of both women. Carlos stood in the doorway for a moment, letting his eyes adjust to the dimness. Next to him stood the man who'd ridden the stallion.

Lee had a moment to inspect him. He was perhaps five feet, ten inches tall, and whipcord lean. He held his hat in one hand and stood calmly, comfortably, the yellow of his hair like a shock of wheat atop his darkly tanned face. A smear of dried blood clung to his cheek, but the rest of it had been scrubbed away. Lee sensed a certain ease about the man, as if he were quite sure he could handle anything or anyone who confronted him. It wasn't arrogance, she decided, nor a practiced front he'd developed. But just *what* it was confused her and made her a little uneasy.

As Carlos led Wade to the table, Lee saw that Bessie's gushing about Wade's eyes hadn't been exaggerated. They were a piercing and direct cobalt blue, and Lee speculated they could probably become diamond-hard at times.

"Miss Lee Morgan," Carlos said, "meet Wade Stuart."

Lee smiled up at Wade. "Please—pull up a chair. Let's talk for a few moments."

Wade grinned, revealing almost startlingly straight and white teeth, a rarity among men in Burnt Rock, and probably the whole of Texas. "Pleased to meet you, ma'am," he said, sliding a chair over from an adjacent table.

Bessie stood, suddenly red-faced. "I'd better work to get back—get back to—" She halted and quickly added, "Good seeing you," as she hustled off.

"Miss Bessie," Wade said to the girl's back. Then he sat across from Lee as Carlos pulled up another chair to the small table. The bronc man's eyes met and locked with Lee's for a long moment. Lee thought she saw the hardness she'd perceived earlier, but she wasn't quite sure.

"Carlos has offered you a job with us, Mr. Stuart?" she asked.

"Yes, ma'am, he sure has. I just wanted to know a bit more about your place, what'd be expected of me, and so forth. And, to tell you the truth, I think Carlos was a bit light on the pay."

"Let's get back to the salary in a moment, Mr. Stuart. We're offering you the job of top hand, and we'll compensate you fairly."

Wade nodded. "Yes, ma'am. But I'm a bronc man, and I don't do anything but break and train horses. You can call me a top hand or call me a prairie dog, but either way I don't do anything but work with horses. I don't hang fence, I don't paint barns, I don't dig wells, and I don't clean stalls." He hesitated for a moment. "I'm not meaning to sound pushy, ma'am, but those are my terms."

Lee met his eyes again. "Are you quite sure you're good enough to make demands like that, Mr. Stuart?"

"Yes, ma'am. I'm sure." He smiled, and the grin seemed to wipe ten years off his face. For a moment he looked like a grammar-school boy. But Lee knew he meant what he'd said.

"I see." She let a minute pass. "Are you interested in working for the Busted Thumb, Mr. Stuart?"

"I'd give it a try, Miss Morgan," he said carefully. "As long as we understand each other and the money is decent. Thing is, I'm not sure what your operation is all about."

"I can fill you in on that," Lee said. "What I'm attempting to do is create a new strain of western horses bred exclusively for ranch work. They need to be fast, intelligent, and very quick on their feet. They need cow sense. And they need endurance, Mr. Stuart. My horses must work hard for long periods of time under the worst conditions the West can offer them. Most of all, my horses need heart."

Wade looked uneasy. "No offense, Miss Morgan," he said, "but do you . . . well . . . know what you're doing? Crossing blood in horses has caused more harm than good for lots of—"

"I'm sure you've heard of Morgan horses, Mr. Stuart."

"Sure . . . but what . . . ?"

"My uncle—the man who raised me—is Noah Morgan. He's a great-great grandson of Justin Morgan, who brought the Morgan horse breed into being. Noah was the finest horseman I've ever met, and I lived with him and his family since I was six years old. And I worked by his side at his horse operation for many years, until I went off on my own—with his blessing. I know horses, Mr. Stuart—perhaps even better than you do."

Again, the disarming grin spread across Wade's face. "Can't ride them like I can, though," he said. He let that comment settle for a moment and then asked, "How much and what kind of stock do you have now? Where are you in finding the cross you're after?"

Lee glanced at Carlos and nodded. "Why don't you answer Mr. Stuart?" she said.

Carlos cleared his throat noisily before speaking. "We 'ave almost two hundred horses now, mostly mares an' geldings, an' maybe sixty colts an' fillies still at their mama's side. We 'ave thirteen stallion. We thin' we 'ave what we want. We very close to breeding the best ranch horses in Texas."

"What pays the bills while all this breeding is going on?" Wade asked.

"We sell the mares and stallions that don' work out, and sell trained geldings for ranch work. Ees a good business—a strong business."

Just then, Lee caught Bessie's attention and motioned her over to the table. "Coffee, gentlemen? Lemonade?" she asked. Carlos asked for coffee; Lee and Wade requested lemonade.

The silence at the table was a comfortable, contemplative one while they waited for the beverages. When Bessie, her face once again a bright red, had brought the drinks, Lee took a long sip. Then, abruptly, she asked, "Are you interested in the job, Mr. Stuart?"

"I am, ma'am. I surely am. Thing is, Carlos offered me only forty-five dollars a month."

"What do you think your services are worth?"

Wade drank the lemonade, wiped his mouth with the back of his hand, and smiled. "More'n you or anybody else can pay me, Miss Morgan. But I'll sign on with the Busted Thumb for fifty-five dollars a month, assuming the grub's decent and the housing comfortable."

"Done, then," Lee said. "Fifty-five dollars a month. Carlos's wife, Maria, is our cook. You won't find better food anywhere. You'll find the tenant house quite acceptable too."

"That's just fine, ma'am," Wade said, rising from his chair. "It's a deal, then."

"One more thing, Mr. Stuart."

"Ma'am?"

"The Busted Thumb is a decent and proper ranch. I've given my life to the Lord, and so have Carlos and Maria. We pray together most evenings, right after dinner. You're welcome to join us. Some of the hands do, and some don't."

For the first time, the young man appeared flustered. "I thank you, ma'am. But I don't think I will. No disrespect intended."

"That's completely up to you," Lee said, smiling to soften her words. "There are a few rules, though. I don't allow whiskey or beer on my land, and I don't allow men to have lady visitors. There's no gambling and there's no cussing or taking the Lord's name in vain. We're honest in all our dealings with each other and with customers."

"That's all fine with me, Miss Morgan. I'll collect my things from the hotel, then," Wade said, turning away.

Lee held out her hand. "One more thing, Mr. Stuart. You're wearing a gun belt and you have a knife tucked into your left boot. I saw the handle when you were riding. No weapons are carried on my land by those who work for me, except when it's absolutely necessary."

For a moment, Lee again thought she saw a cold, flinty spark in Wade Stuart's eyes, but if she had, it was gone as quickly as it had come.

"You're the boss," he said. "My Colt's only for rattle-snakes and coyotes, anyway." He smiled at Lee and Carlos. "I'll be back here in ten minutes or so."

As Wade walked to the door, Carlos spoke quietly to Lee. "Don' need no fancy bone grips on a peestol to shoot rattlers with," he said.

"And no knife in a boot either," Lee added.

# 2

Marshall Ben Flood closed his Bible, leaned back, and sipped at the mug of tea Lee had prepared at the beginning of the evening. The mid-August heat was oppressive, and the air in Lee's parlor, usually stirred at least slightly by a night breeze, was heavy and listless.

"There's more in Leviticus than I ever realized," Ben said. "Reminds me of how little I really know about Scripture."

Lee smiled. "It's not like a mathematics book, Ben," she said. "The Bible is alive—just as all the words of Jesus Christ are alive. Scripture's a big part of any Christian's life."

"Or should be, anyway," Ben answered ruefully.

Lee smiled again, thinking of how she had been more than a little surprised to discover over a year ago that Ben was a practicing Christian. His acceptance of Jesus Christ seemed incongruous to Lee. After all, he was a lawman who'd killed in the line of duty, who ran a tight town, who wore a Colt .45 in a holster that rested low on his right leg, tied down gunfighter-style with a piece of latigo. And he looked like a hard man: tall, lean, and muscled, with shoulder-length dark but graying hair and obsidian eyes that looked as if they'd observed far too much violence and pain for any one lifetime. But Lee had also seen Ben's eyes soften and glint with quick laughter.

Lee took comfort in the fact that she wasn't the only one to have faulty first impressions. Ben had once admitted to her that he hadn't known what to expect when he'd first heard of her operation coming to Burnt Rock. He'd never met a woman who owned and ran a horse farm. Would she be the wife of a rich man, playing with horses a few hours a week between cotillions and dinner parties? Or a rough, crude, and flinty woman who had to prove to herself and to everyone else that she was better than any man? But when he'd introduced himself to Lee in the café, he'd known within a half minute that his preconceptions were terribly wrong.

"How's your bronc man workin' out?" he asked as Lee began clearing the cups and teapot from the table.

"His work is excellent, Ben. He's out there before the sun each morning, checking the stock he's working with, doctoring them like they were little children, handling them, talking to them. I've never seen a better trainer, and I've seen more than a few of them. He . . . well . . ."

"He what, Lee?"

She hesitated for a moment before speaking. "It's just that I don't know a thing more about him today than when I hired him over a month ago. He doesn't visit with the other men at all. I've invited him here for dinner a couple of times, just as I do with all my new hands, but he turned me down—politely—both times."

"Could be he's just a loner. Carlos said he was in the war. Lots of those fellas came home changed—and haunted. The Rebs had boys of fourteen and even younger fightin' toward the end." He shook his head sadly. "I just can't imagine what seein' an' bein' in the midst of those battles would do to a boy's mind."

"I suppose. But still—there's something, well, *dark* about him. I'm nervous having him around, to tell you the truth. But his work is so good, and it's not as if he's done or said anything wrong."

Ben stood and moved his shoulders, as if to ease some stiffness. He met Lee's eyes. "What is it? You're not one to spook like this."

Lee shook her head. "I just don't know . . . except that there's something about Wade Stuart that makes me feel . . . vulnerable, maybe."

"You're a little afraid of him," Ben observed quietly.

Lee stiffened, and the mugs and teapot in her hands clinked together as she did so. "I'm not—" she began heatedly and then stopped abruptly. "Maybe. I don't really know."

"I'll talk to him."

"No, Ben! Please. Leave him be. If there's any trouble, I'll come right to you—you know that. After all, maybe the strangeness is with me rather than with Wade. All my other hands are so much like family here, maybe I'm just not used to a . . . a . . . Wade Stuart. Maybe I'm just being silly. Let it go, OK? At least for now."

"If you say so. At least for now."

They stood together near the rail in front of the house where Ben had hitched his tall stallion, Snorty. The moonlight was soft, diffused by the humidity in the air.

Bats swooped about almost invisibly, gorging themselves on the mosquitoes and other insects in the air. Laughter, rich and warm, floated from the bunkhouse. Ben tightened the cinch of his saddle and wiped his hands on his denim pants, turning to face Lee. He extended his hand, and she took it.

"I had a real nice evening, Lee. Thanks."

Their hands stayed together a heartbeat longer than was required for the sake of courtesy.

"Thanks for coming," Lee said as their hands parted. "And about that other thing we discussed—don't worry. All right?"

Ben stepped into his stirrup and smiled. "Worryin's my job."

Lee watched the marshall ride off, then stared into the night long after she could no longer see him.

The next morning, both a quick, drenching rain and Jonas Dwyer showed up at the Busted Thumb Horse Farm. A dapper man of sixty or so, Jonas was well dressed as always, revealing his age only by the snowy whiteness of his hair and the weather-scribed lines on his broad face. His body was barrel shaped and hard with muscle, his legs were rather short, and his head appeared to sit directly on his shoulders, without benefit of a neck. His operation, Dwyer Horses and Cattle, encompassed eight hundred acres about fifty miles north of Burnt Rock.

"Whoa!" Jonas sputtered as he wiped the rain from his face with a white handkerchief when Lee met him at her front door's small porch. "Ain't this a toad-choker!"

"Jonas," Lee laughed. "Come in, come in! It's so good to see you!"

Jonas stepped inside and extended his hand to Lee. "Always good to see you too, Lee," he said, smiling. Lee stepped past his hand and embraced her old friend warmly, soaked duster and all. Despite his wet clothes, he smelled as he always did—of barber's bay rum, good leather, and pipe tobacco. Lee eased back from him, her hands still on his shoulders.

"I don't get to do that often enough, Jonas," she said. "I don't see why you have to be such a stranger."

"*Me* a stranger? When's the last time you sat at my table, Lee Morgan? Don't you have at least one of those pups you raise that'll carry you to my place without caving in?"

"Sometimes I wonder," Lee laughed. "Take off that duster—we'll have coffee and biscuits in the kitchen." She took his hand. "Please remember me to Margaret. She's been in my prayers. Has there been any change at all?"

Jonas shook his head. "Some days are better'n others. You know how she's been since we lost Stephen. Now the doc says she has some kinda disease that makes older folks confused and forgetful. An' she's takin' an awful lot of this medicine she says helps her. But she's a good woman, an' she's put up with my nonsense for better'n thirty-five years. I owe her at least that many years of care and love."

Jonas settled himself into the chair closest to the stove and mopped his face with his handkerchief once again. Lee gathered up mugs, plates, and biscuits from the warmer atop the stove, then took a large crock of peach preserves from a cupboard and put it and a butter knife on the table in front of Jonas. After she poured the coffee, she placed a mounded plate of warm biscuits within reach of them both.

Jonas closed his eyes and drew a long breath through his nose. "I can't imagine a finer smell to a man who's been ridin' since well before the sun," he said. "I spent the night at Linc Grummond's ranch and lit out early." He opened his eyes and reached toward the plate. He carefully spread peach preserves on the biscuit like a mason spreading mortar, then took a bite that consumed half the treat.

"How has your stock weathered the summer?" Lee asked, stirring honey into her coffee.

Jonas swallowed. "Good. I lost a couple of nice mares to a slew of cottonmouths they stumbled into in a wash, and a few longhorns to rustlers that hit me one night, but everything's good. My foals are growin' like weeds in a garden. Maybe if they'd quit playin' in the lower twenty acres outside my office window, I might even get some work done. They're somethin' to gawk at, Lee. I was always partial to a foal, ya know."

Lee smiled. "I know. And your cattle?"

"Rollin' fat an' rank as a nest of hornets. There's just too many of 'em, an' they're spread out too far. The bulls are gettin' crazy 'cause they don't see a man on horse-back for a month, an' they'd just as soon put a horn in one when they do. I gotta sell off maybe a third of the herd an' consolidate the rest of 'em. Even the cows are gettin' so wild my boys can hardly work 'em."

Jonas took a long gulp of the still-steaming coffee, almost as if he were drinking cool water. He grinned when he saw the alarm on Lee's face. "An ol' cattleman learns to drink his coffee hot an' fast, Lee—he's got to, or he won't get much of it. Always somethin' on a drive that needs attention right this second." Jonas took another biscuit from the plate. "An' the Busted Thumb?

29

How're things here? You gettin' any closer to that horse you're lookin' for?"

"Things are fine here." She put another biscuit—the last one—on Jonas's plate. "We've got a good crop of foals too, and several show promise—show what I'm after. I'm getting closer to the perfect ranch horse. Then my farm will really take off."

"Ol' Slick still the star of the show?"

A smile spread across Lee's face when her friend mentioned Slick, her prime stallion. "He sure is. I'm only breeding him to my best mares, of course, and my Clover birthed a fine colt of his a month or so ago."

"He's a rare stallion, all right," Jonas commented. "'Bout as hard to handle as a fat kitten."

Lee laughed. "A couple days ago, Slick jumped his paddock fence and wandered into Maria's garden. She chased him away, swinging a basket of carrots and peppers at him. It was a picture, Jonas! A five-foot-tall little lady shooing away a thirteen-hundred-pound stud horse with a basket of vegetables!"

"That's a good one," Jonas agreed, his laughter loud and deep. After a moment he asked, "Carlos is well? And your other men?"

"Carlos is as feisty as ever, and all the men are fine. I hired a new bronc man not long ago. Maybe you know or have heard of him—Wade Stuart?"

"Hmmm . . . no, can't say that I know him, and I don't think I ever heard his name neither. An' I know most of those boys. Probably a young buck, right? He workin' out OK?"

"He's young," Lee agreed. "But he's great with the horses. One of the best rough stock riders and trainers I've ever seen—even including the men who worked for Uncle Noah. Wade keeps to himself—and yes, he's working out very well. My sales have gone up already since he's been training for me."

"Glad to hear it." After a pause, Jonas went on. "That's one of the reasons I came to visit. Seems to me that neither one of us is sellin' enough horses. I move some every year, an' I'm glad to hear that you do too, but we simply ain't doin' this right."

"I . . . I don't understand . . ."

"Here's the thing, Lee. The army is gonna be buyin' lots and lots of horses to use in puttin' down all the Indian trouble. Plus, ranchers are cryin' for good, dependable stock that can work a full day an' won't spook every time a tumbleweed blows by. I have those kinda horses, and so do you. But we ain't gonna sell 'em unless people know about 'em. See what I mean?"

"Well, sure. But what's your point? What do you suggest we do?"

"What I think is this: Burnt Rock has a big festival comin' up at the end of September—the Harvest Days Festival. I think we both need to have horses there—our best stock—and show 'em off. Kinda let people know how good our horses are, get people interested. Maybe rent some stalls at the blacksmith's shop. My boys could have a ropin' contest—that always draws folks."

Lee sat back in her chair, thinking, her coffee mug in her hand. "Your idea is a good one," she said, "but we need to take it a couple steps further. It's not Burnt Rock folks who'll buy more than a few of our horses—it's the army and the ranchers, like you said. We can print up flyers and use the telegraph to let the army forts and the big spreads know what we're going to do in Burnt Rock during the Harvest Days. Let them know we have the best stock in Texas." She was hooked on the idea. She spoke faster. "It'll work, Jonas. I know it will! We

don't have much time, but there's enough if we get right
to—"

"'Course it'll work! An' you're right about contacting
ranchers and the cavalry. They'll show up in droves,
looking for good horses an' good buys!"

"I'll get to work on the flyers," Lee offered.

Jonas held out his hand. "One more thing: We need
a big draw, like the main act of one of those circuses
that travel around puttin' on shows."

"Such as what?"

"A race," Jonas said. "A race is how these people test
horses, Lee. You know that. We could run Slick against
my Pirate for a good long stretch—maybe ten or fifteen
miles, or even longer. That'll bring the army and the
ranchers. I guarantee it."

The excitement left Lee's eyes like water rushing from
a teapot. "Jonas, I don't think a thing like that is really
right—not exactly what the Lord wants from us. It's
*gambling.*"

Jonas shook his head. "I'm sorry, but I think you're
100 percent wrong. The race would show both horses
at their best. Whichever of them wins don't mean a hoot!
The point is to get men in a position to buy horses to
see what we have."

"Jonas . . . I'm really sorry."

Jonas waited for a long moment. Then his eyes and
Lee's met and held. "I'd never ask you to do somethin' I
thought was against your beliefs. You know that. But if
we were farmers tryin' to sell crops, would it be gam-
blin' to show our bales of hay or our tobacco or cotton
to buyers, just like all the farmers do at Harvest Days?"

"People don't bet money on whose hay smells sweeter,"
Lee said.

"There are people who'll bet on what side of a gold eagle will come up when it's flipped, Lee. People gamble on cards and roulette wheels and whether or not it'll rain next Sunday." He maintained her gaze and continued. "I learned a long time ago there ain't much I can do to cure all the wrongs in the world, 'cept do the best I can in my own life. 'Course, some men will lay a few dollars on Pirate or Slick, just like men do whenever two horses run against one another. But that don't make what we're doin' a bad thing nor a sinful thing. Not by a long shot."

Lee broke eye contact and took a sip of her tepid coffee. "I'll need to think about it."

"Sure you will. But let me ask a question before I leave. Was your uncle Noah honest, ethical, a good Christian?"

"You know that he was all those things, Jonas! Why would you ask a question like that?"

Jonas smiled. "Do you recall when he ran a Morgan stallion against a great, tall Tennessee Walker at the state fair in Virginia? You were about eight at the time—I remember how excited you were. Noah an' I laughed about what you might do if the ol' Walker won out over the Morgan."

The memory forced a small smile onto Lee's face. She sighed. "I can't give you an answer right now. Can we talk again tomorrow morning?"

"Of course," Jonas said, disappointment creeping into his voice. "That'll be fine. I've some banking and other errands to do in Burnt Rock, and maybe I'll have dinner with Ben Flood. I'll stay at the hotel and ride out here again in the morning. Fair enough?"

"Fair enough," Lee said. They stood at the same time, almost as if on a silent signal, and walked to the door.

33

Lee gave Jonas another hug when they were out on the porch, then looked around her. The rain had stopped, and the air smelled fresh and pure, as if the breeze had swept across a pristine lake. Already, though, the sun was burning off the raindrops that glinted in the grass like scattered diamonds.

Jonas looked down at his hands, as if he didn't quite know what to say. "Until tomorrow, then," was the best he could do.

"Until tomorrow," Lee repeated.

Lee's work that day failed to bring her the joy it did every other day. The morning rain had scoured the air to a purity that not even the merciless power of the sun could diminish, and her horses looked sleek and agile, the hues of their coats sharp and clean against the verdant grass and the blue panorama of the sky. But Lee barely noticed this. She rode past a five-acre pasture where eight foals played under the watchful eyes of their mothers, running headlong, challenging one another, scrambling through impossibly tight turns with unbridled exuberance. Ordinarily, she would have spent fifteen minutes or so simply watching the youngsters at play; today, she rode past the pasture without slowing the gelding she was riding.

She found Carlos inside the breeding barn, doctoring a bruise on a pregnant mare's fetlock by applying a glutinous, foul-smelling paste to the area with his bare hands. The warmth of his fingers and palms and the heat of the injury turned the paste into a liquid that clung to the mare's skin over the bone. Lee dismounted and ground tied her horse, tugging lightly downward with her reins, signaling the gelding to stand still until she returned to him.

Carlos greeted her with a smile. "See the size of thees lady, Lee? Her baby gonna be a beeg one—a strong one."

Lee nodded and attempted to smile. Carlos looked back at the mare's leg and asked, "Ees a problem?"

"Maybe. I'm not sure. Jonas was here earlier—he asked after you and Maria. He has an idea to help both of us sell some horses and make contacts with people who will be return customers." She briefly explained Jonas's proposition.

Carlos's face lit up like a lantern on a dark night. "Ees splendid idea! The army, the ranchers, they use many horses but don' breed their stock—they always need more. An' when Slick beat Pirate, the soldiers an' ranchers, they knock on our door, no?"

"Well . . ."

"Lee, how can you worry? Slick the fastest!" Carlos said.

"I'm just not sure that racing is *right*, Carlos. Men will bet money on the horses. Will that make the Busted Thumb an occasion of sin?"

Standing from his crouch next to the mare, Carlos wiped his hands on an empty grain sack, considering for a long moment before he spoke. "Men bet on horses since forever. If two men each 'ave a horse, one day they gonna race. Ees the way of men an' the way of horses. There ees no way you can control that. But running horses to see who ees stronger an' faster, that ees not a bad thing—ees a thing of beauty an' pride."

Lee didn't respond.

"Look, Lee. Many times you 'ave seen our horses challenge one another an' run together to see who wins, no? Ees a natural thing for a good horse with a lion in hees heart to run against another. God created horses, no? An' *you* know better than God what horses should do?"

Lee couldn't help but smile. "There's some illogic there, my friend. But I see what you mean."

"Illogic? Ees no illogic. Ees the truth!"

"Have you ever bet on a race, Carlos?" Lee asked, grinning.

"No ees *importante*."

"Did Maria find out?"

Carlos's silence was all Lee needed. "How did she feel about you losing the money?"

Their eyes held for a heartbeat before they both broke into laughter. Lee walked back to her gelding, gathered the reins, and mounted. She waved to Carlos and turned toward the south pasture, still chuckling.

"A race ees no a bad thing, Lee," he said to her back, loud enough for her to hear. The laughter was gone from his voice.

That evening, Lee rode Dixie to her favorite vantage point, from which she could view a good part of the Busted Thumb. She dismounted, ground tied the old mare, and walked through the grass to a small depression in the side of a gentle hill that she'd discovered on a previous trip. The ground was softer there, and the water that gathered from the morning rain had long since drained off or evaporated.

Lee had prayed here before. The peace seemed to clear her mind, to allow her to be closer to the Lord by being close to a bit of the calm beauty he had created. She stood still, watching scribbled lines of dry lightning far off in the western sky. The quick flashes grew brighter as the sun dropped below the horizon and darkness deepened. For the first time since Jonas had arrived at her door, Lee felt her tension, her concerns, lifting from her as fog lifts from a valley touched by the sun.

She sat there for quite a while; it was fully dark when she walked back toward Dixie. The mare, happily cropping grass, nickered as Lee attempted to brush the dirt and blades of grass from the knees of her culottes. She accomplished little beyond transferring the mess from her knees to her hands. Giving it up as a lost cause, she rubbed her palms against Dixie's saddle blanket, gathered the reins, and swung into the saddle.

The stars were huge against the unending depth and blackness of the sky, and although the moon wasn't quite half full, there was plenty of light to make riding at a slow canter comfortable and safe. Lee rubbed the side of Dixie's neck lovingly, feeling the liquid ease with which the aged but healthy muscles moved under the mare's sleek hide.

Lee rode back to the barn with her reins looped around the saddle horn, letting Dixie pick her own way down the slope.

Lee was all ready for her friend's return the next morning. The breakfast she was preparing was a special one, and the heat from her kitchen stove permeated her home, carrying the teasing fragrances of the meal. She hummed as she worked, barely able to contain her excitement.

Jonas's boots thumped on the porch as the coffeepot in Lee's kitchen began to boil. The aroma of the Arbuckle's Ground Premium Coffee she'd scooped into the pot filled the room and extended throughout the house like a welcoming smile.

Lee embraced her friend at the door and, before he could speak, said, "Come on, Jonas—I've got something to show you."

Jonas followed her to the kitchen, sniffing the smell of the coffee.

"Sit," Lee commanded, placing an empty mug by the plate, knife, and fork in front of him. "Ham and eggs are warming along with the biscuits. Coffee'll be ready in a minute."

Jonas began to speak, but Lee held up her hand to stop him. "I'll be back in a second," she said as she left the kitchen, heading to her small office adjacent to the parlor. When she returned, she spread a large sheet of paper on the center of the table in front of him. He smiled like a child on Christmas morning as he read it.

### HORSES! HORSES! HORSES!
**The Finest Horses in West Texas Will Be Offered for Sale at the Burnt Rock Harvest Days Festival Sept. 30!!!**
**A RACE WILL BE HELD BETWEEN**
**DWYER HORSE & CATTLE COMPANY'S**
# PIRATE
**AND THE BUSTED THUMB'S SLICK**
**AT NOON!!!**
**Offered for Sale Are Gentled and Trained Ranch Horses, Army Mounts and Remounts, and Riding and Driving Stock.**
**Terms—Cash, Gold, or Good Personal Note**
**HORSES! HORSES! HORSES!**

Jonas gaped at the proposed poster for several moments, then looked up at Lee. "It's perfect!" He stood and eased around the table to face his friend. "You've done the right thing, Lee. This'll be good for both of us and for our ranches. And you sure haven't told a lie here:

We do have the finest horses in West Texas! 'Bout time we let folks know that!"

While Jonas drank a third mug of coffee after packing away a large breakfast, Lee brought paper and pencils from her office to the kitchen table. Together they listed the army forts and encampments within a four- or five-day ride from Burnt Rock, and then they listed the ranches and farms. When they were finished, they'd filled three pages.

"This'll work out fine," Jonas said. "I've got a passel of men who're drawin' pay and not doin' anything but sittin' around waitin' for my October cattle drive to form up and move out. I'll get a few hundred copies of the poster printed at the newspaper office and set my boys loose with 'em—I'll tell 'em to put up a poster anywhere they see another person, even if they have to nail it to a cactus. An' while I'm in town, I'll give the list to the telegraph master and put him to work." He smiled at Lee. "We ain't gonna miss many people."

Lee smiled back. "One more thing," she said. "How long do you want the race to be? A short run won't prove anything to the kind of buyers we're after."

"Like I mentioned yesterday," Jonas answered, "I'm thinkin' maybe ten or fifteen miles, in a big loop toward the hills, where there's some hard riding. We need to show that our horses have heart and that they can cover any kind of terrain without collapsing."

"Fine with me. We can start them right in front of the sheriff's office and send them out Main Street—give the folks something to cheer at."

Jonas nodded. "Can you have Carlos and a couple of others go out and set up markers? Red cloth of some kind would be good. We don't want either rider takin' a turn somewheres and endin' up swimmin' the Rio Grande."

"Sure. Matter of fact, I'll go with Carlos. We'll make sure the way is marked well."

Jonas stood up from the table. "Who's ridin' for you?" he asked.

Lee sighed. "I was thinking about that last night. Much as I'd like to run Slick myself, I don't want to stir up things when there's no need to. So I decided on my new man, Wade. He'll get the job done, and no matter what, he won't hurt Slick. If I put one of my other men out there, he's liable to push Slick too hard if it's a close race. Who are you going to use?"

"Davey Medwin—you know Davey, Lee. One of the best horsemen I've ever met. Been with me almost a dozen years. He might grouch an' carry on a bit if he has to miss the ropin' competition, but he'll put a good ride on Pirate."

As they walked together to the door, Jonas turned to Lee and said, "You need to know this, Lee. Whichever way you went on this racing thing wouldn't have made a tad of difference in how I feel 'bout you."

Lee placed her hand on the man's arm. "I know that," she said. "I'm sure I made the right decision, and I'm comfortable with it."

"Good, good." Jonas paused. "You know, your uncle Noah would be awful proud of you. It would have been a whole lot easier for you to take over his farm after he died an' keep right on raisin' an' sellin' Morgans, instead of chasin' your ranch horse idea. It took some grit."

Together they crossed the porch and walked to the rail where Jonas's horse waited. Jonas mounted. "By the by," he said, grinning, "how does Slick feel about chewin' on another pony's dust for ten miles?"

Lee returned the grin. "I don't know," she said. "And I'm real sure he's not going to find out at Harvest Days."

## 3

"Can he make it?"

"I dunno, Lee. Ees steep. I thin' maybe I call Wade off. The climbs in the race are no like thees one."

Lee and Carlos stood twenty yards from a sharply angled, rock-littered, sandy face that leveled to a plateau at its top. Their horses, picking up on the tension, danced in place, creating tiny explosions of fine dust with their hooves.

Lee watched as Slick dug into the sharp slope, his rear hooves scrambling in the parched soil and churning a thick cloud of grit into the still air, all but obscuring himself and his rider from her sight. Slick's coal-black hide was drenched in sweat, and the sandy dirt adhered to it in blotches and streaks.

Wade leaned far forward at the waist, his head almost touching Slick's neck, distributing his weight to give the horse every possible advantage in the climb. Slick's

41

hooves chewed into the steeply angled ground. Throwing his body forward, he rapidly sucked in air, breathing so heavily that the sound could be heard above the clatter of his steel shoes against rocks and pebbles.

Carlos took a step forward and bellowed, "Stop! He can no do it!"

Lee cupped her friend's shoulder with her hand. "No—it's too late to back away. Let's see . . ." She stopped mid-sentence, stunned at what she saw. She heard Carlos gasp.

Wade must've felt Slick coming apart, must've felt the panic running through the animal's muscles like an electric current. He sawed the reins, fighting to regain control of the horse's head. Then, in a jagged, awkward motion, Wade jammed the reins into his mouth, clenched his teeth on them, and tore off his shirt, sending buttons airborne away from him. Swinging the sweat-darkened shirt up and forward, he settled it over Slick's eyes. Slick squealed and shook his head, but then stopped his crazed headlong rush.

Slick stood, trembling, at an impossible angle on the slope. Wade, still leaning forward, spoke to the horse—or perhaps sang or whispered to him. Lee couldn't be sure. All she heard were soft sounds, some a bit like words, others more like the steady sibilance of a breeze through a field of wheat.

The horse and rider's position was precarious. About two-thirds of the way up the climb, they had another fifteen yards to cover. Pebbles and an occasional rock tumbled and bounced downward, raising puffs of dust as they fell.

Wade eased the shirt to one side and dropped it, still crooning to Slick. The horse snorted wetly as his vision returned. After a moment, Wade straightened a bit and thumped his heels hard against the animal's sides. Slick reacted as nature and the slope demanded—with a surge powered by the awesome strength of his hindquarters. Larger rubble was being dislodged now, banging downward like a miniature landslide. But again Wade used his heels, and again Slick threw himself upward. Wade's back, a pale, almost bluish-white against the bronze of his arms and face, ran with sweat as he urged Slick forward, upward.

Carlos broke the silence. "He weel make it," he said, the words barely louder than a whisper.

On the top of the vicious slope, Slick shook himself, sending off a shower of sweat droplets that glittered in the sun as they fell to the ground. Then Wade was out of the saddle, standing at Slick's head, rubbing his dripping muzzle and again speaking whatever language it was he used with horses.

Lee and Carlos exhaled loudly at the same time. "I've been around horses all my life," Lee said, "and I've never seen anything that even comes near that."

"Me too," Carlos said. Then he spoke through an awed smile. "Slick an' Wade can no be beat."

Lee couldn't disagree. She'd been watching Wade work with Slick for a few weeks now and had to admit that she'd learned a few things about conditioning a horse that even Uncle Noah hadn't known. Even more than that, she was impressed with Wade's temperament—the unhurried, gentle manner in which he handled Slick, and how he seemed to guide the big stallion rather than make demands on him.

Inevitably, during the sessions that ran four hours a day, six days a week, Wade and Slick had run-ins. Slick, with the natural arrogance of a young, strong, healthy horse, sulked at times when Wade asked for a bit more speed or endurance from him. And when Wade reined in Slick when the horse wanted to run his hardest, to cover ground for the pure joy of doing so, there was often a battle of wills. But Wade knew how to handle the stubborn horse. When Slick reared, Wade used the reins to haul the horse's head back to his side so that his nose almost touched Wade's knee—and then held Slick in that contorted position while he worked off his anger in small, clumsy circles.

Lee hadn't anticipated that her stallion would—could—look better than he had before his work with Wade. But now Slick's muscles were as defined and hard as those sculpted in marble by a master craftsman. His coat seemed to glow with a light that somehow emanated from the obsidian black. And the mixture of crimped oats, shell corn, molasses, and a bit of white apple vinegar that Wade fed Slick seemed to be a catalyst that increased his speed and endurance.

And, Lee realized, Slick had come not only to respect Wade Stuart, but to love him. The bond between the horse and the man was as obvious as a thunderstorm, and at times this worried her. She wasn't at all sure how long Wade would stay with the Busted Thumb, and she'd seen good horses become listless, refusing to eat, when a beloved owner or trainer was no longer there. Lee didn't think she could bear seeing that sort of desolate flatness in Slick's eyes.

Less than a week later, at the casual evening prayer group held at the ranch, Lee noticed that the men seemed unusually subdued. The seven men who'd shown up didn't display much—if any—of the spirit that made the meetings such joyous occasions. Even Carlos had little to say. And Rafe, who rarely missed a gathering unless he was riding fence or moving a group of horses to fresh pasture, wasn't there. When Lee asked after him, the responses from the men were mumbled and evasive. Not one of them met her eyes.

Lee glanced at Carlos, who quickly looked away. She knew he was in a difficult position. He needed the trust of the workers and cowboys, and he'd lose that if they believed he snitched to the boss lady about everything that happened out of her sight. On the other hand, Carlos's job as ranch manager and his loyalty to Lee made it impossible for him to keep from her anything she needed to know. But Lee didn't press Carlos in front of the men. She knew he would come talk to her in his own time.

After the meeting had ended, Lee hoped Carlos would remain in the kitchen for another cup of coffee, as he did frequently, but instead he left with the others. She sat at the table alone, listening to the night sounds. Rafe's absence, she felt, had something to do with whatever was going on—and there was most definitely something going on. After twenty minutes or so of forced inactivity and increasing concern, Lee shoved back her chair, stood, and left the house, heading for the grain room in the main barn. She thought she might find Rafe there. One of his responsibilities was to keep the barrels and bins full of feed and to do a check for rodents and snakes at the end of the day.

There were only two lanterns lighting the main aisle of the big barn, but the grain room, situated at the far end of the structure, cast a cheerful splash of illumination into the semidarkness. Lee's boots made almost no sound against the tightly packed dirt floor. When she opened the door to the grain room, Rafe gasped and turned away, fumbling with the sack of crimped oats he was about to heft onto a stack of other sacks.

"Rafe? I didn't mean to startle you."

The man didn't answer. Instead, he grunted as he lifted the sack of grain from the floor, his back still facing Lee.

"Rafe, what's going on? Turn around and tell me."

"Ain't nothin' much, ma'am. I . . . uh . . . I jist . . ."

"Turn around and look at me. That's an order."

The man slowly shifted himself around to face his employer. He was tall and very thin, almost to the point of emaciation. His hands, large and big knuckled, hung awkwardly at his sides, as if they somehow didn't belong at the end of his arms. His left eye was swollen shut, and the bruise around it was a purplish yellow that looked painful under the bright lights of the two lanterns. His nose had grown to a bulbous, off-center knot of red flesh, stretched taut and shiny by the swelling. His lips, once thin, were swollen and cut, and Lee saw a pair of empty spaces in the man's upper front teeth that hadn't been there the day before.

Lee hurried to him. When she touched his arm, Rafe cringed involuntarily and took a half step back.

"Kinda sore is all, Miss Lee. Ain't nothin'." He attempted a smile, but the effort stretched the swollen flesh of his lower lip. A thin stream of blood began its way down his chin.

"What happened, Rafe? Was there an accident? Are you all right?"

Rafe focused on the floor. "Wasn't no accident, ma'am," he mumbled.

"Then what . . . ?"

The man shook his head without looking up.

Lee took a deep breath to calm herself. She struggled to keep her voice even as she said, "Is your nose broken? Are there injuries I can't see?"

"Carlos said it ain't broken. He said I got a couple of cracked ribs. It don't amount to nothin', ma'am. I'm jist fine."

"You're *not* fine, and it does amount to something, Rafe. I'll get Carlos to take you to town in the wagon and have Doc take a look at—"

"No, ma'am. I ain't goin'." Even backed with pain and forced through battered and swollen lips, the words were harsher than Lee had ever heard from him. Then he added placatingly, "Carlos is doctorin' me. Miss Lee . . . I don't wanna talk about it no more. Maybe you'd best ask Carlos any questions you have. It's kinda hard for me to talk about it, an' not only 'cause of my busted-up mouth. Please, ma'am?"

Lee raised her hand to touch Rafe's shoulder and then stopped. She didn't want to see him cringe in pain again. "Sure, Rafe," she said. "I'll talk to Carlos. My only concern is that you're OK. You take a couple days off. I'll tell Carlos. I want you to get some rest—heal up."

Rafe's "thank you" was a strained whisper.

Carlos must've been expecting Lee. He opened the door of his and Maria's small house before she stepped onto the porch.

"I just talked to Rafe," she said. "He sent me to talk to you."

"Come," Carlos said, stepping aside and holding the door. He led her into the parlor, where Maria sat on a wooden chair, sewing a tear in one of Carlos's shirts. She smiled at Lee. "Thees men, they are all loco, Lee."

47

"I won't argue with you on that," Lee said, sitting on the overstuffed Montgomery Ward couch. She looked at her ranch manager. "What happened? Who beat Rafe like that?"

Carlos sat in the chair by the sole window of the room. "I wasn't there, 'course. But I talk to some of the boys who were. It was Wade Stuart who fought with Rafe."

"Fought!" Lee exploded. "There was no fight—there was a slaughter! Wade's much younger than Rafe, and a whole lot stronger!"

"Ees true."

Lee sank back on the couch. "What started it?"

"Rafe, he gave a full bucket of feed to Slick in hees stall—but it was the molasses feed. Wade come in an' see the feed in Slick's bin, an' he throw it out, cursin' an' shoutin.' An' then he went lookin' for Rafe."

"Why in the world would Rafe feed Slick? Wade takes care of all that—not that it excuses anything about what happened, of course."

"Rafe said he forgot. He use to feed Slick every morning and night before Wade come here. He jus' forgot."

Lee sighed. "Where was Rafe when Wade found him?"

"Jus' then he come back into the barn, an' Wade go at heem. The men say Rafe go down, but Wade keep pullin' him up an' hittin' him again. Then he drop Rafe and keek him." Carlos waited a moment. "The men say Rafe din't even fight back."

Lee suddenly felt tired. "I can believe that. Rafe's a gentle man—and a good man too. For Wade to beat him like that . . ."

"I will go find Wade an' fire him, Lee."

"No. I'll talk to him, and if he needs firing, I'll do it."

Carlos stood. "I won' let you go to him alone. Look what he did to Rafe! Suppose he turn on you? No—we go together."

A voice from outside the window stopped all sound and motion in the living room. Maria's right hand halted midstitch, the light of the lantern making her silver needle a shimmering spear of light. Carlos stood as if stunned, swallowing hard.

"No reason for either of you to come looking for me," Wade said from the window. "I'm right here. I figured I'd find you here, Miss Morgan. Carlos, can I come in? I got some things I need to tell you both."

Lee nodded toward Carlos.

"Come," Carlos said, his voice carrying all the welcome of a sudden buzz of a rattler's buttons.

Lee listened to Wade's boots thump across the porch, the door open and close, and the polished floorboards squeak as he entered the small parlor.

"There are some things you don't know about," Wade said. "I wanted to tell them to you before you fired me for beatin' on Rafe."

Lee regained her composure. "Have your say. But I'll tell you this—there's no way you can justify what you did to that man."

"No, ma'am. I don't guess there is."

The bronc man suddenly looked like a youngster facing a very angry teacher. His hands first moved to his pockets, then clasped at his waist, and then separated and awkwardly hung at the ends of his arms. He cleared his throat before he spoke.

"You probably wondered why I keep to myself so much," he began. "Maybe I should have told you this earlier. I got a real bad temper, and it's gotten me in trouble before. I'm working hard on curbing it, and I was doing good until today."

"A bad temper doesn't excuse an assault, Mr. Stuart. Whatever mistake Rafe made with Slick's feed was—"

"Ma'am, Rafe was dead drunk, and he'd been after me all afternoon!" Wade interrupted. "I told him to back off and let me be, but he kept at it, cussin' me and threatenin' me about Slick."

Lee was able to stop Carlos from an outburst by standing quickly and moving to his chair. "I don't believe you," she said to Wade, keeping her eyes locked with those of her ranch manager. "Rafe isn't a drinking man. And I've never known him to curse or threaten anyone."

"He got himself a bottle somewhere today, Miss Morgan," Wade said. "I know that for a fact, and so do the other men who were working around the main barn today. Why none of them went to Carlos I don't know, but what I'm saying is the straight truth. He was drunker than a hoot owl and goading me all afternoon—and when he brought all that rich feed to Slick, I kind of snapped. All that sweet molasses could have foundered Slick—could have wrecked him for the race or for anything else useful."

Lee turned to face Wade. "I want your word on what you're telling me," she said. "I'm going to ask Carlos to go to Rafe right now and ask him about this. If Carlos comes back and says you're lying, I want you off Busted Thumb land tonight—and if you ever come back, I'll have you arrested and jailed. Is that understood?"

Wade looked at the floor in front of him. "You got my word on what I said, Miss Morgan. And I'm clear on leavin' if I'm lying."

Lee motioned Carlos to follow her to the door, leaving Wade staring at the floor and Maria staring at Wade.

"Carlos," she said as they faced one another on the porch, "we need to get to the bottom of this. Talk to Rafe and then talk to a couple of the men. And do it fast, please. What you find out determines whether our bronc man rides out tonight or not."

Carlos nodded soberly. Lee knew he was well aware of the importance of the issue. Good hands on a ranch form an allegiance with one another that demands they protect each other. But on the Busted Thumb, that protection didn't extend to lying to Carlos, Lee, or anyone else.

After Carlos walked off toward the bunkhouse, Lee stood on the porch for a moment, her eyes closed and her hands grasped together at her waist. "Maria," she said as she reentered the living room, "I need to talk to Mr. Stuart privately for a bit. Could you give us a moment, please?"

Maria's glare at Wade indicated quite clearly what she thought of him and of leaving her friend in a room alone with him. "I'll be nearby, Lee," she said.

Lee nodded. "Sit down, Mr. Stuart," she said. "We're not finished here yet."

Wade settled on the edge of the chair Carlos had vacated, his boots planted on the floor in front of him, his hands clasped in his lap. He looked uncomfortable, but he didn't look away from Lee's searching eyes.

"Tell me about the trouble you've been in before," Lee said, lowering herself into Maria's chair.

Wade's voice was quieter than it usually was, and he hesitated slightly after each few words. "Fighting, Miss Morgan. Something would rub me the wrong way, and the next thing I knew, I'd be swinging. It was nothin' real big, but it lost me a couple of jobs a few years back."

"Gunfighting or fistfighting?"

Wade looked as if he'd been slapped. "Never nothin' but my hands, Miss Morgan," he said. "Never."

"What was the last job you lost, and when was that?"

"I was with the Double D way up in Tucson. I came on another hand using a blacksnake whip on a horse, and I hit him some. That was the last time—a little over two years ago. I left Mr. Goodnight on my own."

The sincerity in Wade Stuart's voice was conspicuous—just as it would be, Lee thought, coming from a skilled actor . . . or liar. "What have you done about this temper of yours?"

"I found I do better if I keep pretty much to myself. And . . . well . . . I took it to the Lord and asked his counsel. That helped more than anything else."

"Oh?" It was difficult for Lee to keep the incredulity from her voice.

"Yes, ma'am."

"Are you a Christian, Mr. Stuart?"

"I'm not sure what I am. I guess maybe I'm a Christian. Either way, I know the Lord has been helping me."

The heels of Carlos's boots against the hardwood floor broke the silence that filled the room after that statement. Carlos looked first at Wade and then turned to Lee.

"Rafe picked up a bottle of rotgut the last time he went into Burnt Rock for supplies. He wass drunk today. He claim he don' really remember much about what happened, 'cept that he wass real jealous of Wade spendin' all that time with Slick."

It took a moment for Lee to assimilate what she'd just heard. Then she stood and approached Wade, stopping when she was directly in front of him, looking down into his eyes.

"Carlos and I believe in giving a man a chance to prove himself, Mr. Stuart," she said. "Rafe's drunkenness in no way excuses what you did to him. You should have walked away and explained what was going on to Carlos or to me later. Or saddled up Slick and gone for a ride. You didn't do any of those things." She turned abruptly from Wade to look at Carlos. "How did you leave things with Rafe?" she asked.

"I put a good scare into heem 'bout the booze, an' tol' heem that if it happen again, I would personally chase heem off the Busted Thumb. He been with us over four years with no problems. I don' think there weel be no more."

"Good," Lee said. She turned back to Wade. "You're a good worker and a fine horseman. I wouldn't like to lose you, but that fact won't stop me from cutting you loose if anything even remotely like this happens again. If you raise a hand to anyone on this ranch, you might as well saddle up before the dust settles. That's how fast I'll be rid of you." Lee drew a breath. "Keep that temper in check, Mr. Stuart. That's all. Now go to bed. It's been a long day."

As Wade rose and started to the door, Lee added, "There's one more thing. I'll exercise Slick tomorrow morning. Don't feed him—I'll be out to the barn early, and I'll take care of him when I get back."

Wade stiffened almost imperceptibly, then relaxed. "Yes, ma'am," he said, his voice without inflection or emotion, as calm as it would have been had Lee asked him if he thought it might rain the next day.

After the bronc man left, Carlos sat on the couch and extended his legs in front of him. Lee walked to the window and looked out and around. Wade was gone. She returned to her chair.

"I dunno," Carlos said. "Rafe admitted he had whiskey an' that he wass angry at Wade, but the whole thing don' seem right to me."

"I talked to Wade about his temper, Carlos. He said he's working on it. The both of them acted stupidly today, but we've given men chances before, and we've never been burned."

"So far," Carlos sighed. "But I keep on seein' Rafe's face in my head. A couple of punches don' do that much damage. I guess that's what's botherin' me. Wade went at him awful hard an' awful mean—an' he knew jus' what he wass doin'. I know thees."

Lee sat there for a moment, trying to assemble her thoughts logically in her mind, to sort through her impressions and perceptions of what had happened. *What if Wade had killed Rafe? Is it safe to keep the man on, given what he's done?* She closed her eyes, and the battered face of her wrangler appeared in front of her. *Should I have fired both of them right then and there? Was I too soft because of the work Wade is doing with Slick?*

Carlos broke the silence. "You've not ridden Slick since Wade started with heem?" he asked.

"No. I've missed using Slick, but I wanted Wade to get well into his conditioning before I got up on him again." She smiled. "After seeing Slick on that slope, I'm wondering if he's gotten even faster on flat land than he was before."

"You watch Slick, yes? Maybe he's no so much a pussycat no more. Don' let heem—"

"Oh, hush!" Lee laughed as she stood up. "I'm not going to do anything silly with him. I'm just curious is all."

Carlos walked Lee to the door and opened it for her. "You know what thees curiosity done to meester *gato*—the cat," he said with a grin.

The next morning held the slightest bit of a chill in its still, predawn air—a hint to early risers that autumn was no longer such a long time away. As ever, winter skulked about the corner, waiting impatiently.

Lee preferred to saddle and bridle Slick herself. She hung the lantern she'd carried from her house on a hook outside the stallion's stall and was pleased—as always—to hear Slick huff wetly through his nostrils. His greeting to Lee hadn't changed from the time he first recognized her as a friend and mistress. She fetched her gear from the tack room, breathing in the rich, fresh scent of well-cared-for leather that permeated the small enclosure.

Lee stepped into her horse's stall and latched the gate behind her. She worked Slick's ebony coat with a rough brush, bringing a grunt of pleasure from him. Even at rest, Slick's muscles were long and solid, as if he were a soldier standing at attention.

After placing her saddle blanket carefully on Slick's broad back, she gently smoothed away any wrinkles that could cause abrasions or galls. She tugged the blanket slightly forward to cover his withers and checked once again for wrinkles. Then she hefted her stock saddle onto Slick's back.

Lee felt a stirring of pride for her riding equipment. Her saddle had been crafted by an aged Apache man who'd required almost six months to make it. The price Lee had paid for his work still caused her to swallow hard when she thought about it.

She set the front cinch, waited a moment for Slick to exhale, and then drew the cinch an inch or so tighter. She knew that some horses sucked enough air to launch a dust storm as soon as they saw a saddle approaching them, but Slick wasn't one of those horses. Lee brought the rear cinch together and left an inch of space between it and Slick's belly. The rear cinch wasn't meant to hold the saddle on the horse—its purpose was to keep the saddle from pitching up during rapid turns or sharp descents.

Slick's bit was a low-port, cutting-horse type, with the bar made of brass, which helped generate saliva in his mouth. He accepted the bit readily and without the argument some horses felt compelled to present when being bitted.

Lee swung into her saddle just as the sun was announcing that another day had started. Slick danced a bit, nodding his head, wanting to get moving, while Lee took in the palette of earthy, subdued pastels that were a part of the dawn in the prairies of Texas. Slick snorted impatiently, and Lee turned him toward the trail leading to Burnt Rock, easing him into a canter to let him stretch his muscles and burn off a bit of energy.

When, with her spurless heels, Lee asked Slick to pick up a lope, he stepped into the faster gait with no transition—he *flowed* into his lope as naturally and as effortlessly as water cascades down a mountainside. The impact of his hooves on the soil sounded strangely hollow in the quiet of the morning, and once they were beyond sight of the house and barns, she felt as if they were the only living creatures on earth.

Lee watched Slick's forelegs reach out in front of him and sweep lengths of ground underneath him. *His reach is longer,* she marveled. *I don't know how Wade did it, but he's extended Slick's stride by almost a foot!*

The stallion snorted at Lee, asking for permission to run. Instead, she held him in the lope for another mile until he snorted again, more insistently this time. When Lee gave Slick the loose rein he wanted and leaned slightly forward in the saddle, the stallion threw himself into a gallop. The rush of unleashed power forced Lee to catch her breath in a sensation very close to pure awe.

Her mind flashed on an image that had been with her since she was a child—that of a mountain cat at full run, crossing a valley with the sound of gunfire chasing him. The tawny pelt of the cat had seemed twice its normal length as he covered ground, stretching himself, his belly only inches above the valley floor. Both Lee and her uncle Noah had cheered when the cat made it to the shelter of the trees across the valley as the hunter's last round dug a spout of dirt harmlessly from the earth, yards behind the animal.

Lee cheered again this day—a yell of uninhibited joy at the agility and strength and heart of the fastest horse she'd ever ridden. And her shriek brought even more speed from Slick. He coursed rather than ran, slicing the morning air as a spear would.

When Lee reined Slick in, easing him down from gallop to lope to canter, her face felt scrubbed raw by the air she and her horse had assaulted for the past few miles. Her vision was strained by the flow of wind-generated tears.

She stroked the side of the stallion's neck. He was lightly sweated, and his hide was warm under her fingers. His breathing was regular and not a great deal faster than it had been when Lee first came to his stall that morning. Walking alertly with his ears flicking about, he was interested in everything around him. And when he snorted and tossed his head, Lee realized something that truly amazed her.

Slick was asking to run again.

# 4

Ben Flood halted just inside the swinging batwing doors of the Drovers' Inn, letting his eyes grow accustomed to the murky, smoke-laden light in the saloon. The reek of spilled and sour beer and the sharp, harsh smell of whiskey hit him as if a foul blanket had been tossed over him. The voices of the men at the bar were loud and their laughter raucous. Ben glanced at the card players at the scattered tables, then gazed at the bar. The eyes of the men with schooners of beer and bottles and shot glasses in front of them gleamed drunkenly.

A black man in a suit and a white shirt that was almost blindingly white, even in the feeble light, sat at a piano. Moving effortlessly over the keys, his hands formed chords and rhythms as if it were a natural and uncomplicated process. The musician, freed from the horrors of slavery by the War Between the States, earned a meager living providing what amounted to background noise to the men in the saloon.

The bartender—a huge man built much like the beer barrels he worked with—caught Ben's eyes and raised an empty mug in his direction. "Set ya up, Marshall? On the house, 'course."

"My answer's the same as it is every time I walk into this cesspool. If I wanted to drink swill, I'd go to another pigsty. I don't like this one."

The bartender looked as if he wanted to respond, but when he met Ben's eyes, he obviously decided against it. Instead, he grinned, revealing yellow and broken teeth.

Ben walked through the haze to the piano. "Zach," he said to the musician. "I haven't seen you around much lately."

The man smiled. "I'll tell you, Ben, since I've been playing both shifts in this dump, I haven't had time to do anything I like to do—or should do."

Zach dropped the song he'd been playing and began a lively spiritual Ben was fond of. He smiled as the music rolled out into the surroundings of the saloon. None of the clientele appeared to notice the change in tempo or melody, and no one gave Ben another glance. There was nothing illegal about a saloon, or drinking in one, or playing cards in one—nor, Ben knew, about getting drunk and betting the spring seed money on the turn of a card. But perhaps there would be one day. He hoped so.

Zach then began a muted love ballad that allowed him and Ben to speak without being overheard. Ben casually leaned against the piano, appearing to be watching Zach's dancing fingers on the keyboard. "Anything special going on I should know about?" he asked.

"Lots of money on the race at the Harvest Days Festival. A couple of new cardsharps have drifted in too. Sleazy pair—I'd say they feed each other cards when they get in a game with a few of the boys who've been drinkin' too much. I can't swear to it, mind you, but I'm sure that's what they're doin'."

Ben nodded. "Keep an eye out. If you see anything you can be sure is cheatin', let me know."

"Just like always," Zach said. "They trimmed Danny Morse pretty bad a couple of nights ago. Better than a hundred dollars, all his seed and tool money, is what I heard."

Ben sighed. "Danny's daughter's still sick, isn't she?"

"Part of the money was supposed to go to Doc. He's been riding out to Danny's place every day to tend to the girl. Danny got to drinking in here . . ."

Ben's face and neck showed the rising of his temper, as did a throbbing vein at his right temple. "Are the cardsharps we're talkin' about sittin' in back, at the big table?" he asked.

"That's them," Zach said. "But Ben . . ."

Zach's plea came too late. Ben was already walking to the rear of the saloon. Sitting side by side, the two gamblers had their backs to the wall, a whiskey bottle and a pair of glasses in front of them. Both men had the pallor of those who rarely felt the sun on their skin.

Ben picked up the edge of the table and moved it back. Then he stood in front of the men, looking down at them.

"You boys new in town?" he asked.

"No law against passing through your fine little town, is there, Marshall?" The gambler's smirk said as much as his words did. His partner laughed.

"The reason I stepped over to talk to you is because I want to ask you for a donation for a sick little girl. Her father's name is Danny. I figure a hundred dollars would be about right."

The card players sitting at tables nearby scrambled out of the line of fire, leaving their cards and money behind.

"We ain't payin' you nothin'," one gambler sputtered. "That sodbuster sat down to play cards—"

The other gambler grabbed his partner's shoulder. "Hush up, Bill. I'll take care of this." He reached into his vest pocket and removed two fifty-dollar gold pieces and held them out to Ben. "There's your donation, Marshall. I take it you won't bother us again as long as we're in town, correct?"

Ben accepted the coins and dropped them into his pocket. "This'll go right back to the man you cheated."

The gambler waved his hand dismissively. "Sure, Marshall. You do what you think is best."

"I will," Ben answered. "Now, I want both of you to stand, and I want you to keep your hands away from your weapons."

"We ain't—"

"You'll walk out of here right now, or someone will carry you out. The choice is yours."

After a moment, the gamblers stood and started to walk to the front of the saloon, the marshall a short stride behind them. A few cowboys along the bar watched the parade, smirking, but none was foolish enough to say anything. The gamblers shoved their way through the batwings and out onto the sidewalk. Their faces were scarlet, but neither man spoke.

"You ride out right now. If I see either of you in my town again, it'll be hard on you."

An elderly woman on the wooden sidewalk flashed a toothless smile at the marshall. "Thank you, Mr. Flood!" she called.

Ben tipped his hat to the woman and crossed the street, heading to Doc Palmer's office. On his way there, he glanced into the café and saw Doc sitting at a table with a mug of coffee. He walked in, waving to Bessie, who immediately poured a cup of coffee for him.

The doctor greeted Ben with a warm smile. After the men shook hands, Ben sat across the table from the physician. He tugged the golden eagles from his pocket and handed them to his friend.

"This is against Danny Morse's account," he said.

A look of confusion crossed Doc's face. "But, Ben—Danny lost his money in a card game. I heard all about it. He doesn't have—"

"The cardsharps who robbed him decided to return the money," Ben said, grinning. "I offered to bring it to you." He paused, and his grin widened. "Nice fellows," he said, "but I don't think you'll have an opportunity to thank them. Seems they're leaving town."

Doc Palmer guffawed loudly. "That's a shame. A terrible shame." He pocketed the money. "This'll be a big help. My medical supplier in Chicago cut off my credit again. They don't seem to understand that most of my fees come as a bushel of potatoes, or a couple of chickens, or a fat shoat, when I get lucky."

"I don't guess either of us are going to die rich men," Ben said.

"It's easier for a camel to pass through the eye of a needle . . ." Doc quoted.

"Well, I guess we're in good shape in terms of eternity, then."

Both men laughed.

Just then, Bessie set Ben's coffee in front of him and added an inch to Doc's cup. As Ben sipped appreciatively, he looked around the café. There were a couple of old-timers at a table, and Missy Joplin, a feisty and beloved ninety-year-old widow who'd won the love and respect of the town, sat alone at a table near the window, reading the *Burnt Rock Express* and slurping a cup of tea in the European fashion—through a pair of sugar cubes lodged behind her front teeth. The uncomplicated peace in the little restaurant relaxed Ben, gave him a bit of what he called "room to breathe."

After a moment, Doc said, "Lots of furor about the Harvest Days Festival. Maybe too much, to my way of thinking. I'm seeing faces on the street I've never seen before, and they're not good faces. I'm seeing too many guns worn on a man's leg in gunfighter rigs—and the festival's still a month away."

"I know that," Ben said. "I'm doing what I can to move those types on out of Burnt Rock."

Doc shook his head. "The festival's gotten too big. A few years back, it was women showing their quilts and preserves and pies and men playing horseshoes to win a cake or a dance with a lady. The cowboys did some roping, and the kids ran around, and it was fun and safe and everybody went home at the end of the day tired and feeling good. Now we've got a horse race that's drawing tinhorns and gunslingers and gamblers the way a magnet draws steel shavings. That cesspool across the street is already laying in an extra supply of beer and whiskey. And those booths with contests aren't much but an outright scam. It's no good for the town. If we're not real careful, we'll end up like Dodge City."

"I'm worried too. The last thing Lee or Jonas expected was somethin' like this. They both want to sell some horses and decided a race was a good way to get some attention for their stock. If they'd had any idea of what—"

"I know that, Ben," Doc interrupted. "They're both good and honest people. I'm not pointing a finger at them."

"Well, it's too late to stop it," Ben said ruefully. "People who're comin' will come anyway, race or no race—and I'm not talkin' about families from around here. If there's no race, I think I'd have a riot on my hands."

"What about shutting down the Drovers' Inn during the festival? Seems like that would be a big help."

"I can't do that. I'd need a writ from the governor, and that'd take five, maybe six months to get. As the law stands now, saloons like the Drovers' aren't doing a thing that's illegal."

"It's legal to wreck families and turn good men into stumbling drunks?" The doctor's voice rose in volume and stridency as he spoke. "To suck the money out of the pockets of unsuspecting farmers and cowboys looking for a good time? That's not right, Ben Flood, and you know it!"

"Yeah. I do know it. And there's not a thing I can do about it except try to keep my town as safe as I can and rid it of the men who can hurt my people."

When Doc spoke again, his voice was lower and more controlled. "You're the best lawman this town has ever seen, Ben. Everyone says that. A Christian man with a star on his chest is a rare thing in the West, and we're grateful to have you. I wasn't attacking you, my friend." Doc hesitated and drew a breath. "It's just . . . well . . . I guess I'm as disturbed as you are, seeing these gunslingers and the other no-goods in our town. The merchants feel the same way. Most of them are closing for

65

the festival rather than doing the land-mine business they did in the past. They're scared."

Ben gulped the last of his coffee. "I'll be talkin' to the merchants, Doc. And I'll tell them what I'm tellin' you right now: Nothing like this will ever happen again in Burnt Rock while I'm marshall. All I can do this year is ride it out and keep things as peaceful as possible. But that galls me like a sharp stone in my boot." He sighed and rose to his feet, setting his empty cup on the table. "Speaking of bein' galled, I got a stack of paperwork to do at the office."

Doc stood too. He extended his hand to the marshall. Ben took it, and they shook, almost formally, as if they were sealing an agreement.

As Ben left O'Keefe's and began walking toward his office, a man on a dark bay rode past him. The stranger's Stetson was pulled down low to shade his eyes from the sun. There was a bedroll behind his saddle, but, Ben noticed, no coiled rope at his right knee. His sidearm—an army Colt with ivory or bone grips—rode in a well-oiled holster that was tied to his leg with a length of latigo. Ben watched as the man rode to the Drovers' Inn, swung down from his saddle, tied his horse at the rail, and pushed his way through the batwings.

Pirate seemed as if he weren't touching the ground with his hooves. He ran like a mustang, with his head held higher than many breeds would hold theirs at a hard run, perhaps because his blood was telling him that he needed to be alert as well as fast or he'd never survive.

Still, even with his head where it was, he grabbed ground as if he were starving for it and rolled ahead like a steam engine—fast, strong, an unstoppable machine.

Jonas Dwyer sat on his prized Tennessee Walker, Laddie, and watched Pirate gallop across the fairly level field of pasture adjacent to the Dwyer home. He felt like a fortunate man—a man who'd been blessed with much of what he wanted out of life. He turned in his saddle and let his gaze take in his home and the series of three barns that stood off to the side of the expansive two-story dwelling. A covered porch surrounded the house on three sides, and gliders and cane rockers and chairs were positioned so that guests could visit and talk while enjoying the beauty of the ranch and the wonders of a prairie sunset.

Pirate's deep bay color seemed to be on fire as the early sun touched him. The broad white blaze on his muzzle and his four white stockings were hidden momentarily by the harsh glare. Pirate's rider, Luke, a nineteen-year-old cowboy, had allowed Pirate to stretch at the gallop for a mile and was now swinging him back in a wide, easy loop to where Jonas sat on Laddie. As Luke reined down from the gallop to a lope, Pirate swept over the ground with such consummate ease that it seemed he could hold the gait forever.

Jonas believed Pirate couldn't be beat in a flat race, nor in an endurance test. Never having owned such an athletic horse before, he hoped to pass on Pirate's power and strength and intelligence to new generations of Dwyer stock.

But then he thought about what was going on in Burnt Rock. The possibility that he'd pushed Lee into something neither of them really understood kept him sleepless long after the lamps in his house were extinguished and the ranch was still.

Although he loved the West, despite its shortcomings and problems, he believed himself to be a realist. He

67

understood that the end of the war had unleashed men who'd been forever changed by what they'd seen and experienced. They'd not only become inured to violence and bloodshed, but some had come to enjoy inflicting it on others. Marauding clusters of hard, cruel men gathered together as night riders or donned the cowardly hoods and robes of the Klan, attempting to satisfy what had become a lust for bloodshed. And many of these misfits had come West.

Was he responsible for unleashing such men on Burnt Rock?

Ben Flood had said no—or at least that he wasn't completely responsible. The race, Ben had said, was a mistake, but it was too late to do anything about it. All Lee and Jonas could do was forbid their crews to wager on the race, and then make sure the race itself was run cleanly and without incident. That, Jonas believed, was the easy part. What concerned him was what the riffraff would do to the town and its people.

Luke brought Pirate to a stop a few feet from Jonas. "Sir? You OK?" he asked. "Y'all look like you're lost or dizzy or somethin'. Want me to fetch some water for you?"

Jonas shook his head in an attempt to clear the troubled thoughts from his mind. "No, no, Luke—I'm fine." He forced a feeble smile that he feared wasn't convincing. "Pirate looks excellent," he said. "You're doing a fine job with him."

"Mr. Dwyer," Luke said, "you got nothin' to worry about come the festival. That ol' Slick don't have a chance against our Pirate with Davey on him. An', sir, you can bet on that!"

"That's what bothers me," Jonas said. "The betting part is just what bothers me."

The rattlesnake was a large one, summer-fat from living on prairie dogs and mice it found in and around the barns. Now it was coiled in the corner of a stall, with blood and white flesh showing where the frantic hooves of the mare had kicked and stomped on it. The nonstop buzz from within the thick buttons at the end of the snake's body seemed amplified by the midafternoon silence in the barn. Its head darted from side to side, challenging Lee, who faced it.

The gate to the stall, smashed outward by the mare, gaped wide, its splintered and broken wood telling of the violence with which the panicked horse had hit it. Struggling with the mare, Lee locked her right hand into the halter, attempting to force the animal back from the stall—the one place where the irrational bay had always been safe. Even after her hysterical charge through the gate, the horse felt drawn to this symbol of security, and every time she attempted to lurch into the stall, she shoved Lee closer to the rattler.

A pair of punctures in the mare's chest muscle, both with tiny rivulets of blood meandering down her left foreleg to her hoof, showed where she'd been struck. The other punctures, midway up her throat, bled more copiously. Lee knew the horse probably wouldn't survive, but she wasn't about to let the mare be struck again.

She shoved against the mare and at the same time yelled so loudly that her voice cracked and her throat constricted. "Rattler!" she bellowed. "Help—bring a gun! Carlos—*anyone*—help!"

The horse reared, lifting Lee as it rose, then set her down three feet closer to the corner of the stall, where she could see the reptile's eyes glowing like burning embers in a pitch-black pool. The tempo of the buzzing increased, and Lee could hear the eerie hissing that issued from the snake's widely spread mouth. Jamming her left arm across the mare's eyes, she temporarily calmed the animal—in the young mare's panicked mind, what she couldn't see no longer existed. Then Lee turned toward the rattler.

Its head was as large as a good-sized apple, and its diameter that of Lee's forearm. The two wounds the mare had inflicted on it were no longer bleeding. Any damage done to the snake was superficial.

Lee had encountered snakes all her life—cottonmouths and rattlesnakes, as well as harmless garter and grass snakes. She'd shot poisonous snakes to protect herself and her horses, and she'd helped her uncle dynamite a massive nest of cottonmouths in a small outcropping along the stream that had fed his farm much of its water. But she'd never been this close to a pair of fangs, and her raw fear was sending tiny sparks of shimmering light across her vision. She screamed again.

The snake's diamond-shaped head was no longer weaving. Instead, it was directed at Lee—and Lee knew it could easily strike any part of her. She also knew that while the leather of her boots might hold up against the needle-sharp fangs, her culottes and shirt would offer no more protection than would the wing of a butterfly. Lee looked directly into the rattler's eyes and felt bile rise in her throat.

The mare was panicking again; she squealed, and Lee felt her shift her weight to her haunches. A disjointed but fervent prayer flew about Lee's mind like a bird trapped in a small room. She knew that if the mare reared and lunged again, the rattler would strike. Unable to tear her gaze from the snake's head, Lee watched as a miniscule drop of amber oozed slowly from the tip of its right fang. The venom was the color of good clover honey—and a few drops of it could kill Lee as easily as a stroke of lightning.

The sudden sound of boots thumping on the raked dirt floor of the barn sounded sweeter than any choir Lee had ever heard. The sharp metallic rasp of a shell being levered into the chamber of a rifle made her weak with relief.

"Jus' a second more, Lee," Carlos's voice whispered. "Stay still for jus' a second more . . ."

The report of the 30.30 was immense, ripping the silence into shreds. Entering between the gaping jaws of the rattler, the first slug tore out the back of the snake's head. Its immense body lashed about like a thing possessed, spewing dark streaks of blood and tissue on the stall walls. Carlos fired a second time, and then a third, the explosions pounding Lee's ears like angry fists. The rattler, its death throes over, settled into the straw bedding of the stall.

Lee felt as if she were in a trance when she turned toward Carlos. At that moment, the mare's front legs folded, and she dropped to the floor, taking Lee with her.

A damp, cool cloth in Maria's hand brought Lee back to the world. She looked around, startled to find that she was stretched out on the couch of Carlos and Maria's house. She had no recollection of how she'd gotten there.

"We carry you here," Carlos said, anticipating his friend's question.

As her vision cleared and the memory of what had happened a few minutes ago washed over her, Lee sat up abruptly. "The mare?" she asked.

"She ees dead. She wass heet twice by the snake—on her chest and then on her throat. There wass no way she

71

survive. She went down after I shot the snake, an' she never got up again."

Lee leaned back and wiped the tears from her eyes with the back of her hand. Maria moved close again, her face creased with concern.

"You know thees happen, Lee," she said. "Ees sad, but it happen. The snake keel a good horse an' then he die himself, with Carlos's bullets in heem."

Carlos crouched next to the couch. "Thees mare wass our first snakebite death thees year. Las' year at thees time we had *tres*."

Lee sat up once again, but this time she twisted her legs to the side and put her boots on the floor. The shimmering lights she'd seen in the barn returned for a heartbeat, and then were gone.

"Well," she said. "Well. Thanks for what you did, Carlos. You saved my life."

"*De nada*. I'll have someone check the barns an' stalls every day for snakes," Carlos said. "An' soon the season weel be over."

"The men are taking care of the mare?" Lee asked.

"She weel be buried with our other dead animals. They've moved her, an' they're digging right now."

Lee stood and wavered the slightest bit for a moment, bringing Maria rushing across the room.

"I'm fine," Lee assured her. "A little dizzy is all." She started toward the door, Maria at her side. "I'll see you after dinner?"

Maria smiled and nodded.

A cloud of whitish smoke drifted from the kitchen as the two women passed its doorway. There was a rich, pleasant aroma to it—almost a nutlike scent. Lee looked at Maria.

Maria smiled. "We waste nothing on the Busted Thumb."

Lee swallowed hard and tried to banish the image of the skinned rattler in Maria's pot.

The evening gathering brought in more men than usual, mostly, Lee suspected, because they wanted to make sure she was all right after her run-in with the rattler. Afterward, Lee went to the corral, fetched Dixie, and walked the old horse to the barn to saddle.

Lee knew she couldn't allow the fear she'd experienced that afternoon to affect how she acted or worked around the ranch. Still, she had to goad herself into entering the barn. The front sliding doors were wide open, and the building seemed to be a crouched animal, its gigantic mouth gaping menacingly. *Silly,* Lee chided herself as she lit a lantern. She frowned when she noticed her hand trembling as it brought the match to the wick.

But when Lee arrived at her favorite spot for thinking and praying, the silence and purity worked its usual magic on her. She felt the fear slough away from her, lose its grip on her mind. And the earthy perfume of the grass helped sweep away the stench of gun smoke and blood and panic.

Dixie cropped grass contentedly as Lee left the mare ground tied and continued on foot up the rise to the top of the hill. The silence was so deep that the slightest noise Lee made—her boot dislodging a stone or scuffing against an arid patch of dirt—seemed amplified by the vastness of the prairie.

The evening breeze was as light as a mother's touch on a sleeping infant, barely disturbing Lee's hair. She sat Indian style, looking across the land—the ranch—that she owned. The horses in the various pastures appeared as brown, black, or white irregularly shaped dots, moving about or standing still, seeming as much a part of the land as the grass they stood upon. Lee could see the light in her kitchen and in Carlos and Maria's parlor—warm, welcoming, like the smile of a cherished friend.

The full moon rose while Lee's eyes were closed in prayer. When she opened her eyes, she saw a ghostly, pearl-hued radiance that seemed to come from the ground and rocks rather than from a source impossibly far away in the sky. It was as if the heat and stress of the day had been chased away by a soft light coming from the heart of the earth.

Lee rose and brushed the dried grass from her clothing. Someone on horseback, she noticed, was on the trail from the Busted Thumb toward Burnt Rock. The animal was running hard, but the early dew kept a trail of grit from rising into the air. Even though the moonlight was bright, she couldn't recognize the rider or even the color of the horse.

The image made Lee pause. She'd heard the rumors about the upcoming Harvest Days Festival, about the people who seemed to be descending on Burnt Rock—the type who had no more interest in a festival than they did in studying theology.

Could she and Jonas have foreseen this? No, she didn't think so. The race was simply a device to show off their stock. Horse farms needed to sell horses to stay in business. The army and ranchers and farmers were the largest group of potential buyers, and advertising to them with a competition that matched the best with the best made good sense.

Even so, she felt she should've anticipated the effect the race would have on the town. She'd heard that Ben had fought with a couple of crooked gamblers and chased them out of Burnt Rock—fortunately with no guns involved. And Ben had told her that he'd wired to other jurisdictions, hoping to pick up a few deputies for the duration of the festival. Each marshall he'd contacted had replied the same way: No men available. Those law officers, Ben had told her, were faced with much the same problems he himself faced: insufficient funds to pay personnel, population growth and escalating crime, and drifters and saddle bums moving about the West, bringing bloody trouble with them.

And, of course, it was Ben who had to deal with those violent men—in the streets, in the saloon, and now at the Harvest Days. Lee knew that if Ben were hurt or killed because of what she had set in motion, the grief and the guilt would never leave her.

# 5

The angry crack of two pistol shots and the deep, hollow report of a heavy caliber rifle brought Ben Flood's chin up from his chest and his heels from the edge of his desk. In an instant, he was outside his office, his eyes sweeping the length of the street.

The Drovers' Inn showed the only light on Main Street. The businesses, the café, the livery stable had long since been closed and locked. There was an eerie quality to the darkened street and the hulking, silent structures that lined it on both sides. Marshall Ben Flood knew well, however, that he had nothing to fear from the darkness—the real danger waited for him where light shone out to the street through batwing doors.

The tinkling of Zach's piano had stopped, Ben noticed as he ran toward the saloon, and no sounds emanated from the place—no drunken laughter or curses, no yells or whoops. Ben stopped ten yards from the Drovers'

Inn and took a couple of deep breaths, releasing them slowly. He picked up his Colt .45 until its barrel almost cleared his holster, and then dropped it, letting the weapon settle itself. Next, he walked toward the light and the silence that seemed louder than the usual profane racket that issued from the bar. He hesitated for a moment, standing to the side of the batwings. The time it took to acclimate his eyes to the partial light here and the brighter illumination inside could save his life.

Ben entered the room. Everyone and everything in the saloon was unmoving and silent. Even Zach was motionless, his fingers still poised over the keys.

Ben took in the scene quickly: a man dressed in the black coat, white shirt, and string tie of a gambler stood with his back to the wall at the rear of the saloon. There was a gaping, jagged hole through the flimsy wood about a foot left of his head. The gambler held a pearl-handled Colt in each hand, with the barrels slowly swinging back and forth, pointing like accusing fingers at the entire room. On the floor near the bar, a man lay facedown, either unconscious or dead, a Sharp's 44.40 Buffalo rifle next to him with its lever at half stroke. Under an overturned table, another prone figure lay surrounded by silver and gold coins and a few bills of paper money.

Ben had spent too many years as a lawman in the West to ask what had taken place. The gambler, either cheating or accused of cheating, had been called out by the man under the table. The gambler had taken him down and was fired at by the fellow at the bar with the Sharp's—probably a friend or relative of the first man to hit the floor. Before the rifleman could fully recock his weapon, the gambler had shot him.

77

The silence in the saloon was sepulchral. The slight hissing of the hanging lanterns provided the only sound until Ben spoke.

"Put 'em down and you'll walk out of here," he said. "I'll guarantee that. If these two men on the floor are there because you defended yourself, you'll ride out of Burnt Rock a free man."

"And if I don't put them down?" The gambler's voice was cool and level, betraying no emotion or fear.

"If you don't, you face me," Ben said.

"Seems like I'm facing you right now, Marshall—and it seems like I've got the upper hand."

Ben held the gambler's eyes. Now the twin Colts were trained on him, barrels steady.

"Put down the guns," Ben said. "I don't want to have—"

"Shut up!" the gambler snarled. "I've put more of you jerkwater-town lawmen in the ground than I can remember. You do what I say and you might live through this. You don't, you're dead." A hard smile cut the gambler's face. "If you're counting on help from this bunch of scum, you're even more stupid than most of your mongrel breed. These animals would pick your pocket as you fell, Marshall, and laugh as they did it."

"You going to do something or just stand there and flap your mouth?" Ben's eyes had dropped from the gambler's eyes to his thumbs. His pistols, Ben could see, were double-action weapons, requiring the hammer to be drawn back and then the trigger squeezed in order to fire. Whole graveyards of men had died because they hadn't taken advantage of the newer single-action handguns that came out toward the end of the War Between the States.

But Ben realized the gambler was no amateur. He'd hit the rifleman at thirty feet within a fraction of a second after being fired upon himself—and after dropping the man he'd been playing cards with.

The two Colts were held perhaps a foot apart, the left one slightly higher than the right. The gambler's thumbs rested lightly on the hammers, not pressing against them but maintaining constant contact.

"Here's what we're going to do," the gambler said. "You draw your pistol with your thumb and forefinger and drop it in front of you, and then back away from it. I'm walking out of here to my horse. You understand?"

Ben swallowed hard enough to make it obvious and forced a note of submission into his voice. "Suppose you take me down as soon as I'm unarmed? How do I know you won't do that?"

"You don't," the gambler said, grinning. "Do it now."

Ben's prayer was quick and not fully articulated—more like a flash of a request in his mind—and then time slowed down. He seemed to have stepped back from the confrontation, become an observer, yet he was completely aware of each of his physical motions. He felt his thumb and forefinger tug his pistol upward and out of his holster, and he heard the barrel whisper against the leather. He felt the smoothness of the bone grips as he raised his hand. And he felt his right middle finger move alongside the weapon as he lifted it, and the quick jerk that flicked the pistol to his waiting left hand. The impact between his left palm and the grips made a slight slapping sound, and then the air was thick with gun smoke. The blasts of the three reports sounded almost as one. Behind Ben a slug tore into the wall and another slammed into the ceiling a few yards in front of the gambler as he fell.

"Get Doc!" Ben barked at the string of men along the bar.

"Ain't no reason to do that," the bartender said. "Even Doc can't do nothin' for dead men."

"I said, 'Get Doc.' I meant it."

The bartender nodded to one of the men. "Do like he says."

Zach approached Ben. "Let's go outside for a bit."

The level of noise in the Drovers' Inn increased as soon as the two men left. Before they'd taken more than half a dozen steps, drunken laughter erupted from the saloon.

"Fancy move, Ben. I'm sorry you had to use it," Zach said. "I'd heard about the border shuffle, but never seen it done." There was a long pause as the men walked side by side along Main Street, headed nowhere. "You saved some lives in there," Zach went on. "That gambler was crazy. He'd have opened up on the crowd if you hadn't shown up. You did what you had to do."

Ben stopped and faced his friend. "Times like this, I wonder when some gunhand is going to be better and faster than I am, and I'll be the one on the floor—and if all the men I've killed deserved to die."

"I can't answer that," Zach said gently. "You took the job to enforce the law, and that's exactly what you do."

Ben drew his sidearm, replaced the fired bullets with fresh ones from his gun belt, and held the weapon loosely in his hand. After a moment, he sighed and holstered it. "After a few more years, when Burnt Rock calms down and the West becomes less treacherous, I'm going to quit the law, Zach. And I'll never touch a gun again for the rest of my life."

Zach was silent for a moment, then nodded. "I hope that happens for you," he finally said. "I hope and pray that it does."

They headed back toward the saloon, comfortable in the silence between them.

Then Ben sighed. "I hope nothing else happens tonight," he said. "There's been enough trouble and dying already. I need some time alone."

The telegram was on his desk when he walked back into his office. He read it, folded it carefully, and put it into his vest pocket. Then he went out the back door to saddle his horse. He would get the time by himself that he wanted— for as long as his ride to the Busted Thumb took.

Snorty covered ground effortlessly, his lope as comfortable as the motion of a well-made rocking chair. The night air was sweet, and the scents of the prairie a gentle reminder of the goodness of the earth. But the closer Ben came to the Busted Thumb, the more he dreaded arriving there.

The very edge of the sun was at the eastern horizon as the marshall slowed Snorty to a fast walk and turned on to the rutted wagon road leading to the ranch. Light already flowed from Carlos's home and from the bunkhouse, and a lamp shone through the kitchen window at Lee's house.

Ben rode directly to the barn, dismounted, and stripped his tack from Snorty. He briskly rubbed the horse with a burlap sack from a pile of them in front of an open stall. Snorty grunted with the massage and then snorted wetly as Ben allowed him a half bucket of water and closed him into the stall. The bedding was fresh, and Ben knew it wouldn't be long before Snorty was rolling in it, digging in his shoulders and grunting like a sow pig in mud.

The walk from the barn to Lee's front porch seemed too short to Ben. He approached the door and knocked. Lee opened it almost before the rap of his knuckles died away. The welcoming smile faded from her face as she looked at her friend.

"Ben—what . . . ?"

"Let's go inside," Ben said. "I've got some bad news for you—for all of us."

Lee's hand trembled as she brought it to her mouth. She turned and led Ben into the kitchen. They didn't speak as they walked.

Once in the kitchen, Ben said, "Sit down, Lee."

The screech the chair made as Lee pulled it out seemed as loud as the yell of a mountain cat. "What is it? What's happened?" she asked, her voice breaking.

"Lee . . . I don't know a way to say this that won't break your heart. Jonas was shot and killed yesterday. The marshall from over there wired me, asking me to let him know if I'd heard anything. I'm . . . I'm awful sorry, Lee. He was a good man."

The shock—the sheer impossibility of what Ben had just said—seemed to block Lee's tears. Ben pushed back his chair, stood, and walked to her side. Wordlessly, she too stood, and he put his arms around her, drawing her close. Then the tears came.

Carlos sat at the table, his eyes showing his anguish. Maria bustled about the kitchen, topping off coffee mugs, offering more biscuits or more preserves, touching Lee's shoulder with compassion each time she passed her younger friend and employer. Lee wasn't crying now, but the hint of tears made her eyes glisten. Ben sipped his coffee—the fourth mug since he'd told Lee what happened.

They prayed together, the four at the table, asking for strength and guidance. They spoke about Jonas Dwyer. They spoke about his sense of humor and the love he had for his friends and his employees, for animals, and for the wildness and beauty of Texas land.

Finally, Ben stood, nodded wordlessly to the others, and turned to leave the kitchen.

"Ben," Lee said, calling him back. "I don't want how Jonas died to become common knowledge just yet. Can you hold back the part about him being murdered? And Carlos—don't tell the men about it either—just tell them Jonas died."

Ben nodded. "Sure. Whatever you say."

"Maria and I weel tell no one that our good friend wass murdered," Carlos assured her. "Ben, I'll walk out with you."

In the relative coolness of the barn, Carlos said, "I dunno 'bout the race, Ben. I hate to talk business right now, but I dunno what to do."

Ben settled Snorty's blanket carefully and eased his saddle over it. "I don't know either," he said. "Maybe it'd be best if we shut the whole thing down right now—get out telegrams, make up some new posters." He secured the cinches and slid the bridle over his horse's head. He sighed. "But it's too late. The town is crawling with hard cases now, and there's a herd more on the way."

Carlos nodded. "Wass a bad idea from the start. We should 'ave known . . ."

"It was a good idea to sell horses and give the townsfolk some fun," Ben corrected. "It was my job to realize what sort of men a race between such well-known horses would bring. I failed you and Lee and Jonas and the whole town."

"Ees no true," Carlos protested. "The *pistoleros*—the gunmen an' gamblers—are the trouble, no you or the race. You din't have no way to know."

"Maybe," Ben said, leading Snorty out of the stall and the barn. "But I know the West, and I know how the minds of the gunmen and gamblers work: Where good horses run, the cheats and back shooters cluster like buzzards over carrion, knowin' there's fast money to be made."

Carlos stroked Snorty's neck. "I'll be with you the days of the festival," he said. "I tol' Lee that."

"You can't—"

"Don' tell me what I can no do," Carlos interrupted. "You thin' I'm a fat old man who can no shoot? After thees is over, we'll shoot some targets, no? You see then how a fat *torro* handles the *pistola*."

Ben stepped into a stirrup and swung into his saddle. "Thanks, Carlos." He reached down, and the two men shook hands. Then he turned Snorty and put him, once again, into his mile-eating lope. Burnt Rock would already be wide awake.

The sun fell on horse and rider as if it were determined to melt them both. Ben brought the speed of Snorty's lope down a couple of notches to a gait barely beyond a canter. Still, the horse was dripping with sweat—and so was Ben. The prairie seemed to have no limits. Extending into infinity in all directions, the line of the land was broken only by the occasional stunted cluster of desert pines or patches of dried buffalo grass. The air they pushed through was so still and heavy that it offered none of the slight cooling that ordinarily accompanied motion.

Ben rubbed his hand across his face and shook off the fat drops of moisture. The stubble on his chin was prickly and uncomfortable, and his eyes smarted from the salt of his sweat. Shimmering clouds of heat drifted up from the prairie floor and hung in the air like far-away images of cool water. Ben pinched a bit of Snorty's hide between his thumb and forefinger and then released it. He knew that if the hide were slow to return to its natural state, then Snorty was losing too much water and needed immediate rest. The test showed the horse was doing just fine.

Ben sighed with fatigue. The night before, he'd killed a man he didn't even know, and then he'd ridden miles to bring news of a tragedy to good friends. He recalled for a moment how good it had felt to hold Lee, even under such circumstances, and then guiltily chased the thought from his mind. He hadn't slept in over a day, and he badly needed rest.

He sighed again. The festival and the race weighed on him like a debilitating illness. Trouble was inevitable. Exactly what form the trouble would take was the real problem. There'd be drunkenness and gambling and fighting, of course. But would there be gunplay? He knew that the drifters, confidence men, and gamblers drawn to the race were prone to settle disagreements with guns rather than fists.

He shook his head in frustration. The lawmen in the towns within a couple days ride of Burnt Rock had their own problems. The citizens of Burnt Rock were good people, but merchants and clerks and farmers couldn't be called upon for help in what could become a shooting war.

He reflected on the logistics of the coming race. The course Carlos and Jonas had marked over a month ago was closer to twenty miles in length than the originally discussed ten. The army, as Lee, Carlos, and Jonas had reasoned over coffee in Lee's kitchen, wanted horses with heart, with the ability and willingness to travel over almost any sort of terrain and do it quickly.

The route had several long, barren stretches that on a hot day would send waves of stultifying heat upward as a mirror reflects sunlight. There were no major rivers in the vicinity, but a water crossing at the widest part of a sluggish but year-round arroyo was the halfway point of the course. And there were several hard climbs and difficult descents that could, depending on the weather, be either hard riding if dry or genuinely treacherous if slick with rain.

Ben knew that pure speed wouldn't win the race. The first horse across the finish line would be the strongest, the healthiest, and the one with the most heart—what cowboys and horsepeople referred to as "bottom." The race would be a grueling contest of endurance that would call for skill, ability, and courage from both horse and rider. And the rules stipulated that the riders would not see the course before the day of the race.

There'd be at least three hours, and probably closer to four, between the start of the run and when the winner thundered across the finish line. Those hours would be the hardest ones in Burnt Rock. Liquor would flow steadily at the Drovers' Inn, and the tension generated by the betting and the whiskey and beer would fray the hair-trigger nerves of the gunmen and gamblers. The hard cases at the festival would probably have their own hidden supplies of booze. There was no way to prevent that except to search each man, and doing so would be sure to cause gunplay and bloodshed. Ben had never felt so puny, so inadequate as a lawman.

He reined in and dismounted. He had to hold onto the saddle horn for a moment as dizziness overtook him. When his head was clear, he took off his Stetson and poured two-thirds of his canteen into it. Snorty sucked the water noisily. Ben drank the remaining third from the canteen. The water was flat, sickly warm and metallic, but right then it tasted as good as a tall glass of O'Keefe's lemonade.

Ben swept sweat from Snorty's chest, flanks, and rear with the edge of his hand. The moisture barely touched the parched earth before it was sucked up. He then leaned his head against Snorty's neck and closed his eyes.

He hadn't been able to figure out a solution to his problems, so he turned to God for help. He stood there for a few moments and prayed. When he mounted, the sun didn't seem quite as burdensome.

Wade Stuart lifted Slick's left front hoof and inspected it carefully. Just as he'd found with the previous three, the frog was firm and healthy and the walls of the hoof were cupped evenly and smoothly. The shoe was set perfectly; the blacksmith had done a fine job. Wade gave Slick his hoof back and rubbed his muzzle.

Things had been different around the Busted Thumb that morning. Miss Morgan hadn't been out to the barn yet, and the other men were wondering about that. Carlos hadn't made his morning rounds either, and that confused the men even more. And Wade had heard crying from Miss Morgan's kitchen as he walked to the barn.

He tacked up Slick slowly and carefully, as he did every morning, setting the blanket like a mother covering her child. The horse was antsy; he loved nothing more than a morning run and the hours of exercise that followed it. He snorted at Wade's lack of speed in the preparations and picked at the stall floor with a front hoof.

"You hold on there, boy," Wade said, grinning. "You'll get your workout." As he placed the saddle, the slicker behind the cantle shifted, and Wade snugged the tie strings a bit tighter. Then he led Slick from the barn.

The sky was cloudless and a deep cobalt blue. The hot sun seemed more oppressive than usual, but both Wade and Slick were well used to heat. They'd worked in it every day since Slick's conditioning had begun. Slick paid it no attention, and Wade little more.

Just then Wade noticed Carlos stepping off Miss Morgan's porch and waving him over. Rather than mounting, the bronc man led Slick to the house.

"There ees some bad news," Carlos said. "Jonas Dwyer, Lee's friend as well as mine and Maria's, has died. Lee won' be around much today, an' I won' either."

Wade removed his hat. "Sorry to hear that," he said. When he was mounted, he added, "Give Miss Morgan my regards. I'll stop by later to see her in person."

As usual, Slick wanted to run, and he immediately demanded to do so. The big ebony stallion danced sideways, shaking his head, attempting to capture some loose rein from his rider. Wade chuckled; he enjoyed his daily disputes with Slick, enjoyed his own control of such an awesome amount of power and speed. His hands were gentle on the reins, guiding the horse rather than forcing him. He knew that to get the best from any horse, you must gain the love and trust of that horse. And he knew he had both from Slick.

With a slight bit of leg pressure, he asked for a canter, and Slick bulled into an overly fast and somewhat awkward gait, again asking to run. Wade stopped, made Slick stand in place for a minute or so, and then asked for the canter once again. Slick obeyed this time, but his tail began to spin in anger like the blade of a windmill on a gusty day. Wade laughed at his mount's sulking, wanting the wild freedom of a long gallop as much as Slick did.

They covered three miles at a lope. Slick broke a light sweat after the second mile but showed no more signs of tiredness than if he had simply turned around in his stall. When Wade gave the stallion all the rein he'd been asking for, the initial blast of acceleration was exhilarating, a sensation of almost impossibly fast motion that thrilled his senses.

Wade then walked Slick a mile into a minor canyon cut by the wind, dismounted and loosened the cinch, and led him a few hundred yards before ground tying him in a patch of grass and scrub. Taking his slicker from behind the cantle, Wade carefully unrolled it and strapped on his gun belt and pistol that had been concealed inside. He set the cloth sack of .45 ammunition on the ground. He tied down his holster and stood straight. The fingertips of his right hand, with his arm at ease and hanging casually, touched the bone grips.

A few small cacti were scattered about in the gulch, and dull brown rocks scrubbed free of dirt by the wind littered the sandy earth. Wade walked away from Slick, leaving him grazing on the sparse grass. The brass casings of the cartridges tinkled against one another in the sack as he strode to a position thirty feet from a fat saguaro cactus.

Flexing his right hand, he stretched the fingers apart and then formed a tight fist. When he relaxed his hand, he let it hang for a moment, fingertips caressing the grips of his pistol. Then the weapon was in his hand, spitting six rounds so rapidly that there seemed to be no pause between the reports that reverberated in the canyon around him.

Slick flinched, watched Wade for a moment, and then went back to tugging at the grass. Several weeks ago, gunfire had almost panicked him. Now he paid it little attention.

The cluster of shots in the front of the cactus was small—perhaps palm-sized—but the soft-nosed slugs had torn handfuls of pulp and moisture, green flesh and needles, through the back of the plant, spreading the debris in a thick spray of mush on the dirt and rocks.

After shaking the empty casings onto the ground, Wade reloaded his Colt. The barely discernable *click* as he inserted the last bullet and snapped the cylinder shut pleased him. In his mind, his pistol was a thing of beauty. The front sight had been carefully filed away by a master gunsmith, and the tension on the trigger was reduced to the point where a kitten's breath could unleash a promise of death. The bone grips were carved by a Nez Perce, and it fit the palm of Wade's hand better than any glove could. It was as if the gun were part of him.

Wade reloaded his weapon once again and dropped it into its holster. He walked toward a man-tall cactus, the arms of which grew upward like the supplicating arms of a person pleading for mercy, and stopped twenty-five feet from it. He used his thumb and forefinger to ease his pistol out of the holster and gingerly began to extend it to the imaginary lawman. His middle finger and a flick of the wrist propelled the weapon to his left hand, where the chamber struck his left thumb. He grabbed at the gun again, but caught it by the barrel. Disgusted, he swore loud and long enough to attract a glance from Slick.

It took three more tries to get the move—called the border shuffle by gunmen—right. He'd used it once in Dodge, and it had saved his life. Since then, he'd developed a few new tricks. Again he drew his pistol with thumb and forefinger, barrel pointing downward. His index finger snaked into the trigger guard, and his thumb tapped the grips just behind the hammer. The cactus began spewing seeds and pulp. The six rounds he fired slammed into what would have been a man's chest, had the plant been human.

When the reverberations of the shots died, the silence of the prairie closed in. Wade hated the silence. During times like these, his memories were the most strident. Scenes from Gettysburg deluged him, appeared before his eyes brutally, cruelly, as if he were there again. He saw Emil, the thirteen-year-old drummer boy, flop about on the bloody ground, the Confederate flag he'd carried so proudly a battered rag, pierced by bullets and wet with his blood.

The memory of the army's final charge on the third day of the battle caused Wade's body to shake uncontrollably. The insane, headlong run of the Rebel troops up the impossibly long and exposed killing field ran crazily in his mind. He heard again the waves of rifle fire and cannon fusillades that swept the best and bravest young men of the South to their graves. He choked on the hot, painful breaths filled with gun smoke. He felt the sensation of his boots trampling over the bodies of fallen comrades.

For the first couple of years after Appomattox, Wade avoided silence as much as he could. If he wasn't on a horse, he was in a saloon or in a fight. Now, that had changed. That fury still constantly burned in him. But most of the time, he was able to conceal it from others, even though it was always there, directing everything he planned or did.

Wade Stuart, he believed, had died at Gettysburg. But at the same instant, a new Wade Stuart had been born. The new Wade Stuart's only job, only reason for being, was to exact retribution from the world and everyone in it.

# 6

Lee Morgan felt like a child, alone and frightened.

Her home seemed larger than usual and was filled with a heavy silence. Ben, Carlos, and Maria were gone, and although she'd wanted solitude when she'd had the company of her friends, now the emptiness of her home seemed oppressive.

So much death on the frontier—death in Burnt Rock, death on the prairie. It seemed to her as if the West was so angry that it couldn't contain itself, that it had to strike out. Her eyes rested on the Winchester 30.06 that stood inside her front door. The rifle was as familiar an object in her home as the overstuffed couch in her living room or the cooking stove in her kitchen. An image of the handcrafted little bedside table in her room flashed in her mind. On the table lay a Bible, with a fully loaded Colt .45 in the drawer facing her bed. The weapons were in her home only as precautions, but the stark reality of what they were for struck Lee like a quick slap across the face. *Am I hard enough to live like this? Even the man I'm developing feelings for—strong feelings—deals with violence and death every day, and his pistol is never more than a few inches from his hand.*

Lee began pacing. She stopped next to the table in the kitchen, picked up the coffeepot, and considered putting the cups and saucers and plates into the sink to soak. Instead, she turned away to the window and looked out toward the barns.

*Maybe the frontier isn't for women at all. Maybe it's just too coarse and hard, too deadly and hurtful and full of tears.*

A ruckus broke out in the big barn—horses were squealing, and a hoof thudded against the heavy wood planks of a stall. A male voice thundered above the arguing animals. "Whass the problem here, eh? You wan' I come in there an' geeve you a problem? Hush up now—bot' of you!"

A smile crossed Lee's face even as tears started in her eyes. Carlos's threats to the horses sounded brutal, even threatening—and the man had never raised a hand or a quirt to a horse in his life.

Lee looked down at the coffeepot in her hand. It still contained a cup or so of now-cold coffee. She took her mug from the table and filled it at the stove, sipping, enjoying the harshness as she swallowed. She began to walk again.

Her last conversation with Jonas attempted to force its way into her mind, but she pushed the memory away by thinking of Uncle Noah and Jonas as younger men, when she was still a few years shy of her teen years. *That's where my love of horses came from—the way those two men handled and treated and worked with horses.*

*And the independence of both of them! They were wild as hawks, veering away from what other men did, away from the cities, away from the lives that any sane man would have chosen. Instead, they bred and raised horses and lived on ranches where they were always in contact with the animals they so loved. Jonas and Uncle Noah didn't know the meaning of the word compromise . . .*

"They were men, though," Lee said aloud. "They could . . ."

She walked through the parlor and up the stairs, the creaking of the third and fifth steps as familiar to her as the sound of her own breathing. Her tears ran freely now, and great, hiccupping sobs wrenched her chest. Cold coffee sloshed from the mug she held, and she leaned forward and set it on the floor of her bedroom.

*There's a crossroad here. I need to go one way or the other. If I can't take the frontier, I have to get out. I could sell the ranch and the horses and move to . . . where? A big city? A place where I'd be like other women? If I stay, I'll have to live with being different, being the woman everyone thinks is more than a little strange.*

Lee dropped back onto her bed, her thoughts coming rapidly, pictures and scenes skittering in and out of her mind. She saw herself alighting from a carriage, a superbly dressed gentleman reaching out to her with a hand every bit as soft as her own. She saw herself in a group of other stylishly dressed ladies, sipping tea and discussing the poetry of the British Romantics and wondering when, if ever, the United States of America would be mature and civilized enough to produce such poets. Then Lee saw herself in a steamy kitchen, with pots and pans covering the surface of a stove and several hungry children tugging at her long skirts, whining for attention.

And suddenly, Lee laughed through her tears. The pain in her heart wasn't lessened, but somehow she felt rejuvenated.

This was her life. This was where she belonged.

When Wade knocked on her door that evening, she was sitting in the dark, in the half-sleep state where thoughts are closer to dreams. As she sat up straight from her slumped position, her eyes fought the darkness and a quick yelp escaped her before she could stop it. Jonas had been in her mind, but there was another person too, a man she couldn't quite see. He was on horseback . . .

The knock sounded again, and Lee stood and lit the lamp on the table next to her. She opened her door to Wade Stuart.

His eyes widened. "Miss Morgan . . . are you OK? You look . . ."

Lee beckoned Wade inside. "I was just catnapping," she said, forcing a smile. "It's been a difficult day."

"I know that. I wouldn't have knocked except for the light in the kitchen. I'll stop in another time, Miss Morgan."

"No, no—let's sit for a moment." She led Wade into the parlor and lit a second lamp. Hat in hand, he sat on a high-backed chair in front of the window.

"I'm sorry about Mr. Dwyer," he said. "I didn't know him, but the boys say he was a fine man. I know you were good friends, and I just kinda wanted to say . . . well . . . I'm sorry he got killed . . ." His voice trailed off awkwardly, but he looked into Lee's eyes.

Lee shuddered the slightest bit. Wade's eyes seemed empty, devoid of any emotion. "Thank you for your sympathy," she managed to say.

Then, irritated at herself for what probably had been a trick of the flickering lantern light, she added, "Jonas spent his entire life preparing himself to meet the Lord. He was a good man and a loving man."

"Yes, ma'am. I'm sure he was."

"I'm leaving tomorrow to visit with Mrs. Dwyer for a couple of days, Mr. Stuart. Anything you need from me before I leave? Any problems with Slick?"

"No, ma'am, no problems at all." He paused for a moment. "Carlos is going with you?" It was more an assertion than a question.

"No, I'll be going alone. There's too much going on here for both of us to leave."

"It's kind of a long ride for a girl to go alone, was all I meant, ma'am." He stood from his chair.

"I'm a woman, Mr. Stuart. I haven't been a girl for a long time. I'm as good with a rifle and a pistol as most men and better than many. I'm quite capable of taking care of myself." The words sounded harsh to Lee, so she softened her tone and offered a small smile. "Thanks for your concern, though."

Again, the light seemed to play tricks with Wade's eyes. "Yes, ma'am. Well, I'll be going to look in on Slick and then get some sleep. That sun comes awful early."

Lee walked Wade to the door and then watched him as he strode toward the barn until the darkness enveloped him. In a minute or so, she heard a couple of horses nicker a greeting and saw the white blaze of light as Wade lit a lantern. She closed the door, turned, and returned to the parlor—and again shuddered without really understanding why. She climbed the stairs to her room, doubting that she'd sleep, but knowing she needed the rest.

Lee usually was able to fall into a deep and restful sleep as soon as her back hit the bed. Tonight, though, that bed was a devious enemy, hiding comfort from her. She wrestled with the light sheet that covered her, turning from side to side, refluffing her pillow, growing more wakeful by the moment. And when sleep finally did come, it was sweaty and troubled.

She woke with the first faint light of dawn. The sky was still quite dark, but the darkness had that eerie quality it takes on when the sun begins to threaten it. Scratching a lucifer, she touched the flame to the wick of her lamp and carried the light downstairs.

When she was ready for her journey, she walked out to the barn, carrying a valise and her Winchester. Carlos had Meg, a five-year-old mustang mare with a sweet disposition and an easy gait, between the traces of a small surrey with its top rolled back and down. Carlos also had a steaming mug of coffee for Lee, and he'd placed a pair of freshly filled canteens on the surrey floor.

"I don' like thees so much," he said.

Lee accepted the coffee gratefully, took a long sip, and smiled at her friend. "Don't be such an old woman! I'll be with Margaret before dark."

Carlos grunted noncommittally as he checked the load on Lee's rifle and slid the weapon into the boot behind the driver's seat. He took an army Colt from where it was tucked inside his belt and handed it to Lee. "Thees is for in your bag. You can reach it queekly, no?"

Lee began to protest and then saw the set of Carlos's jaw. She took the pistol and slid it into her traveling bag. Meg snorted and stomped a forefoot, impatient to get started, so Lee stepped up to the driver's seat and unwound the reins from the brake lever.

"I'll stay a day and drive back on the second," she said to Carlos as she finished her coffee and handed back the mug. "Quit your worrying and take care of the ranch." She grinned.

"I should ride with you," Carlos grumped. "Ees not safe—"

"Of course it's safe! I'll see you in two days." Lee lightly tapped the reins on Meg's back, and the mare started ahead, jerking the surrey a bit in her haste to get moving. Carlos called *"Vaya con Dios"* as Lee turned the rig down the dusty path to the main trail.

The prairie swallowed Lee and her surrey; within twenty minutes, she could see only the rutted trail she followed and the awesome vastness that surrounded her. She wondered if there would ever come a time when there were enough people in the West to shrink the hugeness of it, so she could see signs of homes and farms and ranches and good roads where there was now nothing but cactus and tumbleweed. She doubted it; the immensity of Texas was almost beyond human comprehension. And she couldn't think why people would come to this area. Few places had adequate water to sustain life, much less support the needs of a farm or a livestock operation. There was simply nothing here to draw people and the cities they'd build. Nothing.

As she was thinking on this, a shallow puddle of black liquid ahead sent gleaming shards of sunlight at her, and she eased Meg to one side to avoid the muck. *Strange,* she thought. *There seems to be quite a few of those puddles around.*

Lee alternated Meg's gait between a canter and a fast walk, giving the mare long periods at the walk between much shorter stretches at the canter. At midday, Meg showed no signs of fatigue, and she grazed contentedly when Lee pulled in to rest at the shaded side of a slope. The silence around them was profound. It was as if the sun had baked all the sound out of the air, so that not an animal, a bird, or anything else could penetrate the stillness.

She stepped down from the surrey, the biscuit and thick chunk of bacon she'd brought for her lunch in her hand. The small, cold meal that she washed down with now-tepid water tasted as good to her as prime beefsteak and a mound of mashed potatoes would have, and she gave silent thanks for the food. Then she scanned the lifeless horizon. The deep blue of the sky was unbroken by even the least trace of a cloud. There was water a few miles ahead, Lee knew—a sinkhole that had warm and muddy-tasting water, but water, nevertheless. She'd let Meg drink sparingly there.

Lee looked back at where she'd come from. Beyond Burnt Rock, the ruts she'd been following had died out. For the last couple of hours, she'd been traveling due east, using the sun at her shoulder as a guide. Occasionally, she'd come across the desiccated remains of wagons and, more frequently, discarded furniture that'd become too burdensome for the animals pulling the loads. The skulls of cattle—and those of horses too—scrubbed white by the wind and the sun protested mutely against what they and their owners had endured. At one point, Lee had reined in, then straightened and packed some stones and dirt around a wooden headstone that read in deeply gouged letters:

**Our Baby Timothy Homer**
**8-27-75–8-29-75**
**Rest in Peece Foraver.**
**Homer and Marian Stoddard**

When Lee and Meg arrived at the sinkhole, Meg had no problem with the temperature or the taste of the water. Lee let the mare suck for a few long moments and then pulled her head up and away. Meg snorted once and danced sideways a bit, but didn't fight Lee about leaving the water behind.

Lee looked around her and noticed a light tan haze that could have been three miles ahead—or ten. She knew distances were difficult to gauge with only the sun and a few hills to use as reference points. The dust seemed to hang still in the air until she focused and concentrated on it. Then she saw that it was moving slowly but inexorably in her direction. She grinned. *Maybe the prairie isn't quite as uninhabited as I thought it was.*

It wasn't until she saw an outrider far ahead—more of a moving speck, really—swing back and head in the direction from which he'd come, that Lee felt any sense of disquiet. *Why did that rider change directions so abruptly? Why would he need to report back about a single surrey with only one person in it?*

When, after a dozen or so minutes, the tan cloud moved more quickly toward her, Lee swallowed hard and felt moisture between her palms and the reins. She chided herself for anticipating trouble where there probably was none, but she couldn't dislodge the quick spike of fear. As the cloud moved closer and became more distinct, Lee brought the rifle to her lap. A moment later, she tied the ends of the reins together and dropped the loop to the floor, placing her boot on it. She levered a round into the rifle's chamber, set the safety, and again rested the weapon across her lap. Then she leaned forward and tugged her travel bag closer to her feet, putting the Colt within reach.

As the riders topped a hill, Lee could see that there were five of them. Apparently, they saw her at the same time she saw them, because they adjusted their direction more tightly toward her. She checked Meg to a walk. There was nowhere to run—and no reason to even think about running. The men could be some cowhands headed to a ranch, or some travelers, just like her, going to visit a friend or a loved one. She told herself that there was nothing to be worried about. Looking for trouble made no sense at all.

She took deep breaths to calm herself. *Just some travelers—that's all.* She shifted the 30.06 a bit so that her right hand could fall directly to the trigger guard and her left to the forepiece if she dropped the looped reins again.

Just then, the men, as if in a practiced maneuver, put more space between one another. Now they rode ten or so feet apart, and as Lee watched, the distances between them slowly continued to widen. She could see that they wore slickers and carried rifles in saddle scabbards. They didn't look grubby enough to be cowhands, and they didn't have coiled lassos attached to their saddles to the right of the horn, which is the cowboy signature. Their hats—nicely creased Stetsons that were in decent condition—looked too good to belong to range workers as well. And each of the men was clean shaven. The horses they rode, she noticed, were good ones with wide chests and proud head carriage.

The riders stopped in a wide arc fifteen feet from the surrey. One of them, the man in the middle, walked his horse another few steps toward Lee. He was tall, with an angular face and high cheekbones that spoke of Indian ancestry. He smiled, and she saw that his teeth were white and even. But the smile seemed as false as a thief's promise, and his dark eyes had no life in them.

"Lonely out here, ain't it, ma'am?" he asked. The other men chuckled.

Lee held his eyes but didn't speak. The farthest two men were out of her peripheral vision, and she didn't like that at all.

"I asked you a question. I expect an answer when I ask a woman a question." His smile broadened into a leer. "'Specially when she's as pretty as you."

"You've got no call to stop me," Lee said. "This is the end of the conversation. I'll be on my way." She leaned forward as if to pick up the reins, but when she straightened, the barrel of her 30.06 pointed at the man's chest. She thumbed off the safety, and the oiled *snick* sounded as loud as a gunshot.

"You're liable to hurt yourself with that, ma'am. I want you to toss it on the ground right now. Hear?"

"Take your men off to one side and let me pass, and we'll have no more trouble," Lee said. She was proud that her voice sounded strong and confident. "I can use this, and I will if I have to."

The man smirked. "You don't count good, little lady. There're five of us, an' there ain't but one of you. Seems like I'd be givin' the orders." He waited a moment and then added, "'Specially since the two boys you can't see have their long guns aimed right at your pretty head."

Lee swallowed. She'd heard no sound of rifles being drawn from scabbards nor safeties being released. Still, a cold sweat broke out at her hairline. Her mouth was dry as she spoke. "A snake can't do much damage when its head is shot off," she said to the man in front of her. "If I fire, it'll be at you—and you'll go down. Then I'll tend to the others."

103

A bead of sweat hung for a moment in Lee's eyebrow and then slid into her eye, but she fought against the urge to wink it away. She refused to break her glare at the man closest to her.

His laugh was as contrived as his smile. "Feisty, ain't she, boys? The thing is, I'm thinkin' that Winchester is gettin' awful heavy. Pretty soon, the little lady ain't gonna be able to hold it up quite so straight."

"I'll fire it before that happens," Lee said. "You can just bet on that."

"Me an' my boys don't bet on nothin' but sure things, ma'am." He moved his head to scan his followers. "Ain't that right, fellas?"

A voice to Lee's left—out of her line of sight—answered with a coarse laugh. "We sure ain't ridin' to Burnt Rock to buy us a quilt!"

Lee noticed that the voice was loose and the slightest bit slurred. *Good,* she thought. *He could be drunk. He'll be slow . . .*

The leader's shoulders slumped, and he exhaled loudly. "Well, it's clear you ain't got the time to chat with us, ma'am. I'm right sorry you was inconvenienced. Why don't you just go on your way, an' we'll go on ours. Fair enough?"

Lee nodded but didn't lower the rifle. The man had been right: The 30.06 seemed to have the weight of an anvil, and her left wrist and arm were threatening to cramp from the continued stress.

"One thing I'll warn you about, though, back that way . . ." He motioned with his right arm toward where he and his men had come from. "There's some—"

Lee shot him in the left shoulder. The derringer that had suddenly appeared in his hand flew in an arc onto the prairie floor. Thrown from his saddle by the impact of the heavy bullet, the man landed on his back, a patch of crimson spreading around the jagged hole in his duster. Lee jacked the lever of the rifle and spun to her right, firing almost without aiming at the man who was bringing up his handgun from his holster. The slug took him in the left arm with enough power to twist him from his saddle.

Lee jacked another round and turned to her left without lowering the rifle. She'd been correct: The man who had been out of her sight was fumbling for his long gun with clumsy, drunken fingers. He immediately raised his hands. The other two, those in front of her, raised theirs as well. The head man sat in the dirt, cursing, his left arm hanging limply at his side with blood seeping from the wound. Lee motioned with her rifle barrel for the drunk to move closer to the others in front of her. The rider to her right, like his leader, was sitting in the dirt, attempting to stop the flow of blood from his arm.

Lee lowered the 30.06 to her waist but kept the barrel moving, slowly sweeping it back and forth over the riders. She was sure they were gamblers, not only because of the derringer the leader had concealed in his sleeve, but also because of what the intoxicated one had said about riding to Burnt Rock.

"I didn't instigate this, and I'm sorry it happened," Lee said. "Thank God no one had to die here today. You said you were heading for Burnt Rock, and there's a good doctor there. He'll fix your wounds—all you need to do is stop the bleeding until you get to him. I'm going to go on now. If you take another try at me, I won't shoot for arms and shoulders." She lowered the rifle to rest across her lap and picked up the reins. A thought flitted into her mind. "By the way, the marshall in Burnt Rock, Ben Flood, is my husband. Maybe you've heard of him—about how he tracked down and killed the man who murdered his father. That took him a long time, but he did it—and he did it in a fair fight."

When Lee mentioned Ben's name, she saw a quick flash of recognition in a couple of the gamblers' eyes. The cold hand that had been grasping her heart suddenly let go.

Meg was more than ready to leave the guns and tension behind. Lee had barely raised the reins when the mare hustled forward, starting the surrey with a jump that almost dumped Lee from the driver's seat.

After a half hour, Lee's hands finally stopped trembling, and by then a sense of guilt had taken over. She'd shot two men—and only her first round had been aimed. The slug could well have taken the man in the head or heart. And, of course, she'd lied—lied out of fear and a sense of self-preservation, but lied nevertheless.

Had she fired too quickly? Would the head man have shot her? Or did he merely want her to drop the rifle? But, if so—then what? She had nothing worth stealing besides her weapons. She had some clothes that weren't new and a few dollars in cash. Meg, as good of a horse as she was, wouldn't bring fifty dollars at an auction. The surrey was a decent rig—a Studebaker—but nothing fancy. What did they want?

The answer was clear to Lee, and she shuddered at the thought.

She eased the surrey to a stop, rubbing the back of her neck. She'd been looking over her shoulder so often that she'd developed a stiff muscle that burned like fire. She'd seen nothing but her own dust for an hour, and then she'd seen the cloud of grit the gamblers put into the air as they rode away from her, heading to Burnt Rock and Doc's office.

She set the brake and climbed down, then walked a few yards to where a cactus stood, its thick arms reaching upward. There she closed her eyes, lowered her head, and clasped her hands at her waist.

Jesus came to Lee as he always did when she called out to him—more as a dove than a lightning bolt. She let the Lord's words flow through her mind and heart and offered to him her fears and guilt. Then a soft warmth that didn't come from the sun enveloped Lee, and her heart was suffused with a sensation of God's great love for her, like the love of a father for his child. Her fear and self-accusation dropped away as the gentlest of rains falls from the sky, leaving her feeling refreshed and renewed—and safe. She felt as safe as she'd ever felt, as safe as she did when on the hill by the Busted Thumb where she went to pray and to think.

Now she had the strength to continue on.

She hit the Dwyer Horse and Cattle Company pasture when the sun was finishing its work for the day, still offering good light but letting the world know it would soon be dark. Scattered groups of eight or ten longhorns tugged at the buffalo grass, barely looking up as the surrey passed. The cattle in these pastures, Lee knew, were used to people on horseback and wagons and carts. Those on the far-flung pastures of the ranch, however, were as wild and cantankerous as wildcats. Jonas's cowhands always had their work cut out for them when they gathered in these cattle for branding every fall. Lee had helped out one year, doing what the cowboys called "brush popping"—chasing half-wild longhorns out of

107

gullies and canyons where they'd scattered in search of good grazing.

The cattle she passed looked good; they had weight on them, and Lee saw no running eyes or the listlessness that signaled a sick animal. A massive bull that seemed the size of a steam locomotive, with horns extending a foot on each side of his head, trotted toward the surrey, snorting a challenge. He lost interest quickly when he realized that neither the horse nor the driver had any interest in him or his harem.

She rode in sight of Jonas and Margaret's home, a sprawling two story that had been added to over the years as more space was needed. Built over twenty years ago when Jonas and Margaret first came to Texas from Virginia, their home had a texture of peace and permanence to it. Mary, the Dwyer's oldest daughter, had moved away from home almost fifteen years ago when she married a doctor with a brand-new diploma. They and their children now lived in Massachusetts. Mary's sister, Janice, lived in Chicago, where her husband was a merchant. The oldest of the Dwyer children, Stephen, had been killed in the War Between the States, near an obscure little town in Virginia called Vicksburg.

Margaret Dwyer had never recovered from Stephen's death. She'd slipped deeper and deeper into a depression that seemed to plague her heart every waking moment. She then discovered patent medicines—elixirs and potions that promised good health and mental clarity. The "medicines" were, in fact, alcohol-, laudanum-, and opium-laden swill that tricked an unsuspecting person's mind. Margaret, Lee knew, was hopelessly addicted to the nostrums and had been for several years.

As Lee drove Meg toward the main barn, Vergil Penn, Jonas's ranch manager, rode out to meet her. Lee reined in and stepped down as Vergil swung out of his saddle. The two hugged. Lee had known the man since she was a child. He had to be well over seventy now, but she had never seen him look so old. Dark hollows hung under his eyes, and his wrists were gaunt, like those of a child.

"I'm so sorry," she said into Vergil's shoulder. "So awful sorry . . ."

"We all are, honey. How such a thing could happen to a man as good and kind as Jonas is beyond me."

Lee stepped back. "What happened, Verge? Marshall Flood said it was a murder. I still can't believe that. Who would ever even think of murdering Jonas?"

The man's eyes filled, and tears spilled down his cheeks. He tried to turn away, but her hand on his shoulder stopped him.

"He was back-shot, Lee. You know how he always had to be out there in the horse pasture. He rode out alone last Thursday mornin', sayin' he wanted to check on a couple of mares he was thinkin' about bringin' in to breed. I didn't think nothin' of it—it's the type of thing he done nearly every day. Maybe an hour later, I heard a shot. It was one of them Sharp's Buffalo pieces—I know the sound of them good enough. I couldn't think of nothin' but gettin' on my horse and hightailin' it to the pasture Jonas went to. I *knowed* there was somethin' wrong, honey, just as sure as I would if the Lord hisself told me there was. I rode hard till I seen Jonas's horse grazin' with his reins danglin' on the ground. Then I seen Jonas." He wiped the tears from his face with the sleeve of his right arm. The gesture seemed almost boyish to Lee.

"Jonas was dead when you got to him?" she asked quietly.

Vergil nodded, swallowed hard, and then spoke. "Yeah. What a Sharp's does ain't pretty, but at least it killed him quick. He prolly didn't even hear the shot."

"Why, Vergil? And who did it?"

"Nobody knows. Nobody. Jonas, he didn't have an enemy in the world. His wallet an' pocket watch was still with him, so it weren't no robbery." The tears started again. "Jonas was a soft touch with anybody with a sad story. He woulda gave money to anybody who asked him. He was always takin' in one stray or another, givin' 'em work. An' then the most of them, they'd steal him blind an' ride off at night—on one of our good horses too. I used to rag on Jonas, tellin' how we needed to put the law after every one of them thievin' skunks." Vergil's voice cracked. "Now I wish I'd kept my mouth shut, 'cause Jonas, he was doin' the right thing, just like the Bible says."

"C'mon, Verge," Lee said gently. "Let's walk on into the barn and let me get my mare in a stall. We'll talk as we walk, all right?"

She stepped to Meg's head and slid her hand inside the halter, tugging Meg forward. After a few steps, she took her hand out, and Meg followed along behind her, as a boy's dog follows his master. Vergil led his saddle horse by a single rein.

"Me an' the boys, we buried Jonas up on the hill, jus' like he wanted. The minister came an' talked, an' lots of folks was there. Even a couple of them drifters he helped out paid their respects."

"Was Margaret there?"

"Nah, she wasn't. Margaret's a for-sure mess, Lee. She's skin an' bones an' don't eat enough to keep a sparrow alive. She's kinda in an' out of what's happenin' around her. Sometimes she'll sit there in the kitchen and talk as normal as anyone else, then she'll drift away."

"Does she understand that Jonas is dead? Has she talked about him with you or the minister or anyone?"

"You gotta understand that poor Margaret's been gettin' a whole lot worse in the past few months," Vergil answered. "She sent a couple of my men into the mercantile over in Holland's Crossing and had them buy a bunch of cases of her medicine. She keeps it locked in Stephen's old bedroom, like she's afraid somebody's gonna take it away from her. I figured I should be the one to tell her about Jonas, an' I did, but I'm not sure she got it. She cried real hard for a minute or so, an' then just stopped, an' a little smile come on her face. Then she asked me to make sure Stephen weren't pesterin' the boys to let him ride one of the stallions. She said there's not a reason on earth why a nine-year-old should be around a stud horse."

Lee's tears started again, and she brushed them from her face with her sleeve. "I pray for Margaret every day, and I'll pray *with* her while I'm here, whether she knows what I'm doing or not. And I'll pray for strength for you, Vergil. If anyone can keep the Dwyer Horse and Cattle Company running as it should, it's you."

They walked the rest of the way to the barn in silence.

When they arrived in the barn, Lee looked around. Jonas's barns were as clean as hers, and they had the same wonderful scent of wood and leather and horses. Vergil called a ranch hand and told him to take care of Lee's mare and surrey.

"She's done a good job for me today. Please go very easy on the water. She isn't hot, but I'm always afraid of founder."

"Yessum," the hand said, smiling. "No hoof, no horse. I'll be real careful."

There was no need for him to explain the old horseman's axiom. Lee had heard it all her life. If a horse's hooves weren't sound, the animal was of little value to anyone.

Vergil stripped the saddle and blanket off his horse and began rubbing the tall gelding's back with a piece of burlap feed sack.

"Is Pirate in his usual stall, Verge? I think I'll take a look at him before I go to the house."

"Ma'am?" he asked, as if he hadn't heard her.

"I asked if Pirate is in his usual stall." She looked at him. "What's the matter?"

"I thought you knew, honey. Margaret sold Pirate the day Jonas was killed."

# 7

Ben Flood stepped out of his office and pulled the door shut behind him. He blinked in the bright sunlight, then glanced up and down the length of Main Street—not because he thought something was wrong, but because it was his habit. What he saw stopped him in place. A stranger was riding down the street on Jonas Dwyer's horse Pirate.

Ben looked more closely at the horse, but he knew he wasn't mistaken. Pirate, to a horseman, was almost impossible to miss: The burnished bay of his coat, the powerful lines of his legs, and the depth of his massive chest made him stand out from other horses the way an eagle stands out in a gaggle of geese.

Ben knew that horse theft was a relatively rare crime in the West—primarily because the penalties for it were severe. A captured horse thief's life often ended as soon as the captors came to a tree with stout enough limbs to support the weight of a man and a length of rope. Justice frequently came even more rapidly than that; men on horses they didn't own and had no reason to be riding were often summarily shot and killed.

Pirate's rider, however, didn't look like a horse thief—or at least any horse thief Ben had ever seen. This man was tall enough to look well matched with the horse's sixteen-hand height. He sat in the saddle a bit stiffly, perhaps because he didn't spend enough time there to make it a completely natural position for him. He wore a pinstriped suit, a white shirt, and a foulard tie, and his boots glistened like polished ebony. He reined in when he saw Ben approaching him.

Ben stopped and stood a few yards in front of Pirate, his right hand hanging easily at his side, his fingertips just grazing the grips of his Colt. The sun was at a tricky position—behind the rider and white-hot bright against a clear blue sky.

"Afternoon, Marshall," the man said. His voice was that of a banker or perhaps a judge—authoritative, deep, the type of voice that never had to ask for anything more than once. "Nice little town you have here," he added.

Ben assumed there was a smile behind the words, but he wasn't sure. To look at Pirate's rider's face would be to look straight into the sun.

Three men on horseback who had followed Pirate out of the livery stable hung back, silent, apparently at ease. One had kicked his left foot out of his stirrup and cocked his leg over the saddle horn. Another built a cigarette, his fingers moving with the economy and skill that come with repeating a task thousands of times. The third drank from his canteen, wiped his mouth with his sleeve, and jammed the cork back in, tapping it with the flat of his hand.

"I've seen this horse before," Ben said.

"Oh? Well, he's been around, I suppose. Doesn't seem strange that you'd remember a creature as beautiful as this fellow."

Ben heard condescension in the voice—and the tang of mockery, as well.

"I'll have to ask how you came by him," he said.

Slight creaks of saddle leather and the shuffling of hooves from behind the man on Pirate told Ben that the three men were suddenly very interested in the conversation between the lawman and their friend.

"And I'll have to ask you to get out of my way, Marshall. My name is Harley Botts. This animal is bought and paid for, all legal and aboveboard. You have no right to brace me in the middle of the street like you would a common thief."

Ben kept his eyes moving between the speaker's chest and the group of men behind him. "That's where you're wrong," he said. "This is my town, and I make the rules. I know that horse, and I need to see somethin' that proves to me that you own him. Otherwise, you're goin' to jail."

"Move or we'll ride over you, tinhorn. I have things to do."

Ben took a half step back and spread his boots another few inches apart. His right hand now hovered over his pistol. Botts obviously didn't miss Ben's repositioning. He sighed. "Like I said, he's mine. I've got the bill of sale right here." His hand moved to the lapel of his coat.

Ben's pistol appeared in his hand, its barrel pointing at Botts's chest. He caught a flash of movement within the three-man group. "Don't do it!" he shouted. "This man will go down dead if you do!"

Botts chuckled. "Are you a bit nervous, Marshall? I was reaching into my pocket for the bill of sale."

Ben backed away a few steps, his Colt still centered on Botts's chest. "Take it now—and do it very slowly. Like you said, I'm nervous. If I get just a little more nervous, I'll pull this trigger."

Botts unbuttoned his suit coat and opened it with his left hand. With his right, he reached into the inside pocket and withdrew a letter-sized envelope. He held the envelope out toward Ben.

"Put your boys at ease," Ben said. "There doesn't need to be a fight here."

Botts waved his hand casually, as if brushing away a fly. The tension left the street as the men relaxed, holstering their side arms.

Ben stepped ahead and took the envelope from Botts. After a moment, he dropped his weapon into his holster. The page of neatly folded paper was headed "Bill of Sale." Ben read it carefully.

*On this day I have sold my horse named Pirate to Mr. Harley Botts for the sum of two hundred dollars ($200.00). Cash was paid to me this date.*
*Signed: Mrs. Jonas (Margaret) Dwyer*
*Signed: Harley Botts*
*Witnessed: Luke M. Tryon, Circuit Judge*

"This won't hold up, Botts," he said, struggling to keep the anger out of his voice. "Mrs. Dwyer has been sick for a long time—she's not capable of selling anything to anyone. And this price—two hundred dollars isn't a tenth of what Pirate is worth."

"It'll hold up, Marshall. Mrs. Dwyer has been signing legal documents all along—checks, receipts, bank deposit and withdrawal slips—just like anyone else.

With her husband gone, his property belongs to her. She's free to do with it whatever she wants."

Ben dropped the page and the envelope to the rutted street. "This is dated the day Jonas Dwyer was murdered."

Botts smiled. "Should I have waited maybe a week, so he'd be more dead than he was that day?"

Ben swallowed, choking off the words that were formed in his throat and burning to be released. "I've heard of Judge Tryon. He hasn't had his nose out of a whiskey bottle in twenty years. He had a man hung last year for stealing a pair of horseshoes. He's a crazy, drunken fool, and—"

"And," Botts continued, "he's a duly appointed circuit judge in good standing in the great state of Texas."

It was several moments before Ben trusted himself to reply. "We're not finished yet, you and me," he said. "Not by a long shot."

Botts laughed again, but didn't reply. He motioned to one of his men, who then dismounted, picked up the envelope and the bill of sale, and handed them to his boss. Botts refolded the page, slid it into the envelope, and put it back in his jacket pocket. Pirate danced a bit, impatient, and Botts reined him around Ben and set off down Main Street at a walk.

Margaret Dwyer's smile was disconcerting to Lee—as out of place as a bull buffalo in a Sunday school class. Margaret was a tall woman—five foot, seven inches—and her emaciation was all the more striking because of her height. Her face, once beautiful and full of life, was sallow, with deep pockets below her high cheekbones. Her hair, which Lee could recall as being luxuriously long and a sunny, almost sparkling auburn, was much shorter now and a flat gray color, tugged together

117

in a sloppy bun at the back of her neck. In her right hand, she held a teacup; in her left, the saucer. Lee had once seen a dead Cherokee child who had died from diphtheria. The infant's wrists had been like dried sticks, and that image leaped into Lee's mind as she looked at the wife of her old friend.

"Well, if it isn't . . . how good to see you, dear!" Margaret gushed, the smile remaining fixed on her face as if it had been carved there. She drank from the cup and then set it and the saucer aside on a table in the foyer. She turned to embrace Lee.

Margaret's body smelled gamy and unwashed, and her breath was redolent with the overripe sweetness of rotted fruit. Her frame against Lee's body felt like a scarecrow, and Lee shuddered involuntarily.

Margaret stepped back. "Shall we sit in the parlor and visit?" she asked, sounding like an excited child. "It's time for my medication, but I'll be with you in a moment and we can catch up on simply everything!"

Lee walked quietly to the table in the foyer and picked up Margaret's cup. Even before she raised it to her nose, she was assailed by the strong scent of alcohol and a cloying, heavier odor. She replaced the cup on the saucer and headed to the parlor. She sat in a chair across the parlor from a long, leather-covered couch, where Margaret sat when she entered the room.

"Well, now," Margaret began brightly. "You're going to have to help me out just a little bit, dear. You see, I seem to have forgotten your name. It's right on the tip of my tongue, of course, but I can't bring it to mind. Isn't that awful? I've been so busy, though. I hardly have time to catch my breath."

118

Lee hoped her face didn't show her shock. "I'm Lee Morgan, Margaret. My uncle Noah was great friends with Jonas."

"Of course you are! You and Stephen played together like brother and sister—always sneaking rides on Jonas's horses." She paused and took a sip out of a narrow bottle she had taken from the pocket of her dress. Her hand covered the label, but the smell of it reached Lee almost immediately—the same fetid scent the teacup had offered. "Stephen's not here right now—the boy doesn't stay still for a minute. He's always in the barn or chasing across the pastures after a horse. Why, Lee, I can hardly keep track of him myself."

Lee nodded, unsure of what to say. A silence began and then grew to the point of awkwardness. "I was so shocked when I heard about Jonas, Margaret," she finally said. "He was a wonderful man. We'll all miss him. I wish I could have been here for the service. Carlos and Maria send their sympathy and prayers. They're very fond of both of you."

For a moment, a weak light flickered in the dull depths of Margaret's eyes. She doused that light with another sip from her bottle. "Thank you," she said. "I expect to be moving soon. It doesn't seem right to . . . to . . . be here. I'll sell the ranch and the stock, I suppose."

"I understand you sold Pirate."

"Oh yes, I guess I did. But Jonas had already made the deal with the man. All I did was take the money and sign the bill of sale."

"Jonas would never—" Lee caught herself, lowered her voice, and began again. "It's strange that Jonas sold Pirate. We had plans for a sale of your horses and those of the Busted Thumb, but I never thought Jonas would part with his Pirate. He was planning on entering him in a race."

"A race?" Margaret asked. "Oh yes, the man said he was going to run Pirate in it—said he promised Jonas he would. I forget his name, but he seemed very nice. Paid me in cash. He brought me a bottle of medication too. There was another fellow with him, I think."

"Margaret," Lee said slowly, "I'm not sure you did the right thing. There are people who try to take advantage of a woman alone."

"Alone? Dear, I wasn't alone, and I'm not alone. I have Stephen."

Lee took a deep breath. "Maybe we should have a lawyer come out and talk about some things with us, Margaret. If you're sure you want to sell the ranch, you'll need a lawyer anyway, to make sure—"

Margaret stood quickly. She took a swig from her bottle and then slammed it down on the table next to the couch. "This ranch is not for sale! It's my husband's legacy, and it'll stay in the Dwyer family. Who do you think you are to come here talking such nonsense? This visit is over, miss." She weaved slightly as she strode to the stairs. "None of the land and none of the horses will ever be sold," she added. "And certainly not to a woman I don't even know!"

"Margaret, please . . . I'm not trying to buy anything. I want to help you make some sense out of all that's happened. Please, will you pray with me? Can we seek the Lord's help together?"

The mention of the Lord's name seemed to jog something in Margaret's mind. She stood for several moments with her bony hand on the stairway rail, half turned toward Lee. After a long moment, she said, "I'm very tired, dear. I need to rest." She started up the steps.

Lee stayed in her chair and listened to Margaret's footsteps ascend the stairs and then cross the room directly above the parlor. The silence that followed was only an outward one. In Lee's mind, there was chaos.

Pictures of Margaret pounded through her brain. Margaret pouring cold buttermilk for her and Stephen. Margaret in a silver-garnished sidesaddle atop the horse Jonas had imported from Europe for her. Margaret laughing while Uncle Noah and Jonas pitched horseshoes. Behind each image, Margaret's new voice bellowed with such tremendous volume that Lee feared her ears would explode from the din. *I seem to have forgotten your name. . . . The boy doesn't sit still for a minute. . . . Not alone. I have Stephen. . . . To a woman I don't even know!*

Lee wasn't sure how long she sat in the Dwyer parlor, but when she finally stood, she crossed the room and picked up the bottle Margaret had left on the table. There wasn't much light left; Lee had to bring the bottle close to her face to read the fine print on the label. As she did so, the fumes from its open neck caused her to gasp. The label read:

**Doctor Theophilus Turnwell's Guaranteed Elixir Cure**
**For Nervous and Physical Problems**
**ABSOLUTELY GUARANTEED!**
**Made from the mysterious roots of specially selected**
**shrubs and trees in Africa, Egypt, and Australia,**
**this elixir is a positive cure for sleeplessness, anxiety,**
**all female problems, ruminative thinking,**
**melancholy, and nervous distraction.**
**The patient will see immediate and profound**
**improvement in his or her condition. Sadness will depart**
**within moments of the patient's first dose, and all ailments**
**of the mind and spirit will be banished forever through**
**continued use of this product.**

**DIRECTIONS:**
Mix liberally with tea or other beneficial beverage or
ingest by itself. Drink when required for the ailments or
afflictions cited above. Dr. Theophilus Turnwell's
Guaranteed Elixir Cure is available in economical
cases of 24 bottles per each case. See your druggist.

There was three-quarters of an inch of yellowish liquid in the bottom of the bottle. Carrying it between her thumb and forefinger as if it were a dead rat, she walked to the window and poured the thick, greasy liquid onto the parched grass below. *I know she has more—lots more,* Lee thought. *But it feels sooooo good to do this.*

The night for Lee was a long one. She ate a plate of beefsteak and beans Vergil had brought to her, along with a tall glass of fresh milk, which was a rare luxury on the Busted Thumb since one of the ranch's milk cows died a year ago. Margaret hadn't extended an invitation to her to spend the night, but Lee realized her friend was out of touch with many things, including social amenities. The couch was comfortable, and there was a quilt neatly folded over the back that would make a warm covering. The arrangement would do just fine for a night or two.

Lee found comfort in the night sounds of Jonas's operation, which were much like those of the Busted Thumb. The stomping of a hoof on the floor of a stall, the bark of a dog, the nickering of a mare to her foal were background music that helped her ease into sleep. The only discordant note was the occasional lowing of a calf or cow from the nearest pasture; the Busted Thumb didn't run any livestock but horses and a few chickens for eggs and for the pot. Several times, the cattle sounds jerked her back to full wakefulness.

Once during the night, she lit the lamp from the table in the parlor and carried it with her up the stairs. Margaret lay on her back, fully dressed, on the bed. Jonas's hat hung from a peg just inside the door, and two pairs of polished boots were aligned on the floor below the Stetson. A man's ivory-handled hairbrush, some pocket change, and a tattered Bible were the only items on the top of the long wooden dresser. Lee could see none of the standard grooming aids of a woman, no cut-glass perfume decanters, no cold cream or skin oils, no combs or brushes or ribbons. Next to the bed on a small table, another bottle like the one downstairs stood in the moonlight, a bit less than half full.

Margaret's hands were crossed over her chest like those of a corpse ready for viewing. Lee had to hold her own breath and concentrate her eyes on Margaret's sunken chest to discern the movement that indicated life. The harsh light of the lamp was cruel to Margaret's face; her skin was flat and pale, and the shadows under her eyes made her head appear skull-like. Lee prayed over the woman before going back downstairs to await the dawn. There was no reason to stay longer. She could do nothing for Margaret or the ranch until she returned to the Busted Thumb.

The journey back home was seemingly longer than the one she had made the day before. As she drove the surrey in the hot sun, she thought about what Vergil had told her as he readied Meg for the trip home.

"I dunno what's gonna happen here," he'd said. "I'm hopin' we can sell off some stock at the Harvest Days Festival—maybe take a few dollars less to move horses on out. If the race had went like it was supposed to, it woulda been good for us, but I dunno if Pirate's owner's even gonna run him." Vergil spat to one side as if the words "new owner" left a foul taste in his mouth. "Margaret's gettin' worse—I guess you saw that clear enough. What's gonna happen here without Jonas . . . well, I jus' don't know. I'll keep things runnin' as best I can, but I ain't no bookkeeper or lawyer. The feed bill is due 'fore long, an' the men need to be paid in a couple of weeks. I never had nothin' to do with the money—Jonas, he done all that. Truth is, Lee—" Vergil's ears reddened and his voice dropped a bit. "I never had no time to learn to read or write very good. I can do some figures, but not a lot." He cleared his throat. "I'm wonderin'—could you maybe look into this?"

Lee spent the rest of her trip home composing in her mind the wires she'd send to Jonas and Margaret's children. She wondered if the two sisters even knew of their father's death and decided they didn't. The responsibility of informing them would accrue to her, she knew, and this made her heart heavy. Her decision to send Uriah Daily, her own attorney and financial advisor, to the Dwyer ranch to look after the books made her feel a bit better. Daily's fees would hurt her own budget, but the Lord had provided for her many times before, and there was no reason why he wouldn't this time.

By late afternoon, when Meg perked up as she began to catch the scent of the Busted Thumb, Lee's mind was buzzing with ideas to help Margaret through the storm she was still suffering under.

When the man on the tall, rangy buckskin tied up his horse at the hitching rail in front of the Drovers' Inn, a cluster of men were standing outside, grouped around

Pirate, the only other horse at the rail. The range horses and grade stock of the cowhands and drifters in the saloon had been moved down the street to rails in front of other businesses, in deference to Pirate. One of Botts's men sat on a chair he'd brought out from the saloon, watching over the horse and warning cowboys away when they got too close. Only a couple of the gawkers paid any attention to the buckskin and the man who rode him. Those who did—two men who obviously knew horses—nodded to the rider. "Looks like he can cover some ground," one of them said.

The rider grinned. "I ain't yet found a horse could cover it faster," he said. The man was built like a cowhand: average height, thin frame, a tan almost as dark as the worn stock saddle he rode and the boots he wore. His hair—brown with some gray—sprouted in bunches and clumps from under his Stetson. His denim pants hadn't been new in a long time, nor had the work shirt he wore. There was a rifle on his saddle, but he wasn't carrying a side arm, at least not a holstered one.

"My name's Tim," he said. "I might be interested in runnin' my horse for money." He turned and pushed through the batwings of the Drovers' Inn.

The saloon had more customers than usual for a weekday afternoon, and the crowd was different from the place's usual clientele. Most of the cowboys who'd show up later in the evening were punching cows or stringing fence or digging wells. The men here now were drifters, gamblers, and scammers who crisscrossed the West, seeking an easy few dollars.

Harley Botts sat at the rear of the saloon, his back to the wall. There were two empty bottles of whiskey and a collection of empty beer schooners on the table. Six men clustered around him, mostly strangers to Burnt

Rock. Botts's hat hung from the back of his chair, and his tie had been pulled apart and hung limply on his chest. Several amber stains sullied his white shirt, and he added another as he laughed loudly at a remark he'd just made.

"So," he continued, "I saw this Appaloosa was a good-lookin' horse, well muscled, strong lookin', but I knew he couldn't dust Pirate on the best day he ever had. The sodbuster tol' me his Appy'd never been beat. Well . . ." Botts paused to down two inches of whiskey from his glass. "I jist love to hear those words. I says to the ol' coot, 'My horse can go a bit. I ain't never raced him 'gainst a real fast one like yours, though.' See, the bartender had tol' me that ol' fool had a bank loan right in his pocket, an' he'd had a few whiskeys. I says to him, 'I jist might put my Pirate 'gainst your horse—but I'm gonna need some odds to make it worthwhile.' Well, the ol' boy's eyes lit up like—"

"That your horse out front?" Tim interrupted. "The bay?" His voice wasn't loud, but it cut through Botts's alcohol-drenched narrative as a sharp knife cuts a piece of twine.

Botts straightened in his chair, and his eyes narrowed. "It's my horse," he said. "What of it?" The threat in his tone was dulled by his tongue's stumbling and slurring.

"Is he the one going against the Busted Thumb's Slick in that Harvest Festival race?"

"I haven't decided whether or not I'm running Pirate then," Botts answered. "And either way, I don't see how it's any of your business."

Tim smiled as condescendingly as a teacher would at a child's foolish answer to an easy question. "Can't say I blame you. That Slick is pure lightnin', from what I heard."

Botts pushed his chair back from the table. "That's what you hear, is it? Maybe you know a whole lot about fast horses?"

"Nah," Tim said. "I don't know a whole lot—but I do know one thing: My buckskin out front is faster than your Pirate."

Botts sprayed whiskey out his mouth as he convulsed with laughter. The men around him laughed too. Waving an unsteady but dismissive hand at the man standing in front of him, Botts said, "You're a fool—git away from here. Me an' my friends are busy."

Tim backed up a full step, color spreading across his face. "I guess there ain't but one way to prove what I said, but I won't race my horse 'gainst a boozer who's too drunk to know what he's doin'." He turned from the table and walked to the bar, motioning with one hand toward the beer spigot.

"You!" Botts bellowed, half standing, supporting himself with his hands on the table. "You want a race, do you? Then you got one! An' I'll tell you what, ya hayseed—I'll pay three-to-one odds!"

One of Botts's followers stood, moved hurriedly around the table, and grabbed his leader's arm. "Boss, we ain't even seen this buckskin horse run yet! Givin' odds like those is—"

Botts shoved the man. "You!" he yelled across the saloon. "You got a thousand dollars to back up your big mouth?"

Tim retraced his way to Botts's table. He tugged his shirt free of his pants, revealing a folded leather pouch. From it, he carefully counted ten one-hundred-dollar bills and placed them on the table in front of Botts. "Looks like we got us a horse race," he said with a grin.

In a moment, twenty or more men on horseback had gathered outside of Burnt Rock, twenty yards away from where the buckskin and Pirate danced in anticipation, raising puffs of dirt. The shortest of Botts's men—a grizzled older man with knotted, greasy hair and a face as wrinkled as the shell of a walnut—was on Pirate's back, speaking quietly to the horse. Tim rode his own horse.

Botts stood between the horses, a quart bottle grasped loosely in his hand. When he gestured with it, whiskey slopped from its neck. "That outcropping—maybe two miles or so out—ya both see it?" The riders nodded. Botts stumbled backward, managed to catch his balance, and went on. "I'll count to three an' then say 'Go!' You boys round the outcropping an' come back past me, an' the race is all over. First horse by me wins." He sucked at his bottle. "One!" he roared. "Two! Three!"

On "Go!" the horses hurled themselves forward as if they'd been slammed in the rump with a fence post. Clods of dirt and grit spewed in their wakes. A cheer went up from the watchers as bills and silver and gold coins were changing hands among them.

The buckskin grabbed the lead and stayed a horse length ahead of Pirate when the horses were at full gallop. Both animals broke sweat almost immediately as they pounded toward the jutting shaft of rock in the distance. The buckskin's chest and flanks turned to a dark, almost mahogany color as he struggled to keep his lead over Pirate.

Pirate seemed settled in his position, his nose six feet behind the buckskin's streaming tail. It was impossible to see from where the observers were clustered, but the man on Pirate held a rein so tight that the animal couldn't achieve his full, breathtaking stretch that he exhibited at top speed.

They rounded the outcropping in a half circle, wide enough to keep them from having to change lead or gait, but narrow and tight enough to use as little ground as possible. Fifty yards from the outcropping, the buckskin faltered the slightest bit; he seemed to sway slightly and for a quick moment, his head raised from its greyhoundlike position.

Conversation stopped midsentence in the group of men. Botts, leaning sloppily against the saddle of the horse he'd ridden to the contest, was the only one whose eyes weren't squinting at the approaching two horses.

When the buckskin wavered again, it was more obvious. At the same moment, Pirate's rider gave his horse full rein, and Pirate floated past his opponent.

The old man was stepping down from his saddle, a smug smile pasted on his face, when Tim brought his sweated Appy across the finish line. Tim ground tied his horse, took the folded bills still laying on the table, and held them out wordlessly.

Botts snatched the money like a pig grabbing a snoutful of slop. "Looks like you lost a thousand dollars, hayseed," he gloated. Then his face seemed to harden, and his eyes became those of a snake staring at a cornered mouse. "Now, I'll tell you what: You an' that loser pony of yours git outta my sight, an' don't let me see you 'round here again."

Tim held Botts's glare for a full minute without speaking. Then he reined his horse around and set out at a walk away from the group of men and horses, and away from Burnt Rock.

Botts watched the man and his horse move away and then turned to the audience. "All right, fellas," he slurred, "you come to see a race an' you seen one. I'm buyin' at the Drovers'—an' there's one more thing. Come that race between my Pirate an' that horse Slick? I'm payin' four to one, an' I'll start takin' bets today!"

"Boss!" Pirate's rider shouted. "That's plum crazy. Your booze is talkin' for ya!" He looked anxiously at the others. "You boys wouldn't take a man who's had a couple of sips at what he says, would you? Ain't nobody in the world gonna pay four to one on a race 'tween such good horses. Why, if—"

"Shaddap, ya ol' fool!" Botts roared. "My word is my word no matter when or how I give it! An' boys, my offer stands! Les' git back to town—racin' makes me thirsty!"

Two hours later, Tim sat on his horse behind the livery barn, rolling a cigarette.

"You did fine," Botts said, wearing a fresh shirt with his tie in place. He handed a sheaf of bills to Tim. "Just like you always do."

"My pleasure, Harley," the man said. "You're playin' a drunk better an' better each time you do it." He pocketed the money. "Say, what's up with the four-to-one odds? You gone crazy?"

"Sure—crazy like a fox. That's why I had the ol' geezer hold so tight onto Pirate during the run. Pirate didn't look like a whole lot, and everyone knows that Slick is flat-out fast. Why, Pirate barely beat that ol' buckskin! These boys'll bet a lot more when they think of the odds, and when they're sure Slick can't tow Pirate."

"You sure don't miss a trick, do you, Harley?"

Botts smiled. "No. I don't."

# 8

Even after a short trip away from her ranch, Lee felt great joy upon returning to the Busted Thumb. Of course, there were the multitude of annoyances and problems that any animal operation generates, and things periodically went askew for no reason at all. But the problems were her problems, and that made all the difference.

As she stood in her parlor, sipping at her morning mug of coffee, a motion outside caught her attention. She walked to the window and parted the curtains.

Lee didn't recognize the well-muscled Appaloosa tied to the hitching rail adjacent to her house. She looked at the animal for another moment before responding to the soft knock at her front door. The stranger on the porch was dressed almost formally, she noticed as she pulled the door open.

"I'm Harley Botts, Miss Morgan. I'm the owner of Pirate."

"So I've heard, Mr. Botts," Lee said, unable to keep the chill from her voice. "What is it you want from me?"

Botts fidgeted a bit, his hat clutched in both hands. "I wonder if we could talk inside for a moment?"

"I don't know that we have anything to discuss."

"Ahh—but we do." A quick spark of what appeared to be irritation flashed in the man's eyes and then was gone. "I'd appreciate a few moments of your time."

Lee studied the man for a moment and then stepped back from the door. "I'll give you a very few minutes," she said. He followed her into the parlor and stood until she asked him to have a seat.

*All the snakes in the West don't crawl around in the brush. Lots of them wear fancy suits and talk real pretty. And they're as deadly as an eight-foot rattler.* Lee wasn't sure who'd given her that warning, but it'd stayed with her and often tempered her dealings. She'd found that, along with the good and honest people, the frontier had more than its share of grifters, liars, and smooth talkers who preyed on those who trusted them. She knew it wasn't fair to judge a book by its cover or a man by his clothing, but experience had taught her to be cautious of men with soft white hands and liquid words that flowed easily off the tongue.

Only a month ago, a fellow who could have been a brother to this Botts had appeared at the Busted Thumb in a surrey, representing himself as a veterinarian and offering a line of medications guaranteed to cure any equine ailment. Lee had sniffed the contents of a couple of bottles from his sample case and then briefly quizzed him on some of the more basic diseases and injuries to which horses were prone. The medicines had smelled like concoctions of alcohol and kerosene, and the drummer's knowledge of horses was abysmally non-existent. So Lee had stood from her chair in the parlor, crossed the room, and picked up the Winchester next to the door. The shyster had left hurriedly, without a word.

Botts settled in at the end of the couch as Lee sat on the chair near the window. "What is it you want from me?" she asked.

"Ma'am, I think I owe you an explanation. You probably don't know a whole lot about me, and I'd like you to know a bit more." He grinned at Lee, showing white teeth. "The fact is, I've known and been good friends with both Margaret and Jonas for several years. I'm a horseman, and I'd had my eye on Pirate since the day he was foaled. I made several offers to Jonas—very generous offers—but he always refused."

"Jonas never mentioned you to me, Mr. Botts. Don't you find that a little strange?"

Botts looked perplexed. "Why, yes, ma'am—I surely do find it strange. Jonas and I got together a couple of times a week to gab about horses and simply enjoy one another's company. Why he didn't mention our friendship to you is beyond me."

"I understand you paid two hundred dollars for Pirate. That horse is worth at least two thousand. How do you account for that?"

"The agreement had long since been made, Miss Morgan. Jonas knew how I felt about that animal, and he promised that if anything happened to him, I would be allowed to purchase Pirate for a token price. Jonas said I should give the money to the church building fund, which I did. I didn't have to do that, but I did—out of the kindness of my heart, and just like I told Jonas I would. I also gave two hundred dollars to Margaret

133

when I paid my regrets about Jonas's death. I have a witness to that. My friend, Judge Luke Tryon, was with me."

Lee looked for signs of duplicity in Botts's eyes. What she saw there wasn't so much deceit as a cold hardness, a lack of human warmth. "I'm not quite sure I believe you," Lee said. "And I don't think you rode out here to square yourself with me. You don't seem like the type of man who would do that. So let me ask you again: Why are you here? And what do you want?"

Botts took a long, dark cheroot from his inner jacket pocket and a wooden match from his side pocket. He glanced up at Lee before lighting the cigar. "You don't mind if I smoke," he said.

"I do, actually. Please answer my questions."

Color rushed to Botts's face as he slid the cigar back into his pocket. "I'm sorry this conversation couldn't be more civil," he said. "My reason for being here is to confirm that the race at the Harvest Days Festival will be run as scheduled, regardless of Jonas's death."

Lee's stomach was suddenly queasy, and she felt uncomfortably warm. Sweat sprang from her palms. She knew she was experiencing a physical reaction to Botts. Looking at the man evoked the same sensations that had overcome her when she'd looked at Matthew Brady's photographs of the carnage of the Battle of Bull Run. She swallowed before speaking.

"My Slick will run in that race for a couple of very good reasons. First, the race was something that was important to Jonas, something he worked very hard to arrange. And second, the town marshall tells me that if the race isn't run, he could have a riot on his hands. People who don't belong in Burnt Rock or any other civilized town have been flooding in for weeks. There's a shooting or two every day. People are afraid to walk

Main Street. If the race will get the trash it attracted out of town, it will serve a good purpose."

Botts stood. "Fine, then. We're in agreement." He paused for a moment and then added, "I think you'll find you're wrong about me, Miss Morgan."

Lee stood and led Botts to the door. As he walked past her onto the porch, Lee spoke again. "One other thing. When Jonas owned Pirate, who won the race didn't mean a great deal to me. Now that you own the horse, the winner is important. Slick will beat you, Mr. Botts, and he'll wreck whatever plans you have to enrich yourself at Burnt Rock's expense."

Botts opened his mouth to reply as Lee firmly shut the door in his face.

While Lee's body carried out its duties for the rest of the day, her mind whirled and raced. There was a thought—a concept—that eluded her each time she tried to bring it to clarity. It was there, that idea or whatever it was, but it danced just ahead of her, vague and without form or substance. Images of Wade Stuart flickered in her mind for no good reason as well, and several times she saw him speaking the words Harley Botts had spoken to her earlier.

Later that day, Carlos found Lee standing at the corral gate, staring out into the prairie. "Lee, I think you miss a bad cut on Clover when you look her over thees morning." His liquid brown eyes showed his concern. "Ees a deep cut. I think she need steetches."

They walked to the barn and down the central aisle to Clover's stall. Lee went inside, nuzzled the mare for a few moments, and then checked her left rear pastern. The cut was an ugly thing. A flap of flesh about four inches long gaped away from the laceration, and clotted blood had formed a thick, elevated lump the length of the cut. Flies gathered around the wound, landing on it hungrily. Clover too had been worrying it—the blood on her muzzle was evidence.

"I missed it completely," Lee admitted.

"So, we feex it now. Ees no big deal." Carlos waited a moment and then went on. "But are you OK? You seem . . . I dunno . . . lost, no? Can I help you, my friend?"

"If I knew for sure what the problem was, I'd ask for your help. It's just something I need a little time to work out, I think," she said. She forced a smile. "Don't worry."

"You know where me an' Maria are if you need us."

This time her smile was less forced. "I know. Now let's take care of Clover. We'll need the grain alcohol, some hot water, my needle, and some of the catgut Doc gave us. And gauze too, and that canvas belt. We'll need to wrap the cut well or she'll bother it and stop it from healing."

As Carlos fetched Rafe and assembled what they'd need to sew up Clover's leg, Lee sat on a bale of hay at the far end of the barn and closed her eyes. The sweet, summery scent of the alfalfa hay enveloped her and soothed her as a warm blanket would on a cold winter night. She pushed away from her mind whatever it was that had been eluding her. Instead, she visualized the steps the suturing process would require.

A few minutes later, she crouched beside the mare's injured leg. Carlos had hung a lantern in the rear of the stall. Rafe stood at Clover's head, applying pressure to her stretched upper lip with a twitch—a few inches of smooth chain through which a horse's upper lip is pulled. Lee had seen leg bones set and wrapped when anesthetic wasn't available, all because of the use of a twitch. Without it, the horses would have been panicked with pain.

Lee's suturing needle was made of brass, almost three inches long and slightly curved. Purchased from a veterinary school in upstate New York, it had cost the Busted Thumb twenty-two dollars. But Lee knew it was worth every penny of that exorbitant price. Its tip was sharper than the most carefully honed razor, and it slid through tough horsehide with almost no resistance and very little pressure on the user's part.

She cleaned the laceration with a strong solution of grain alcohol and warm water, probing as gently as possible with a flat-ended surgeon's tool to remove any dirt from the area. With the same tool, she removed all of the clotted blood and then washed the length of the cut again after adding more alcohol to the solution.

When Lee first eased the needle through Clover's flesh, the mare moaned deep in her chest. It was a heart-wrenching, pitiful sound—and Lee paid no attention to it. She knew there was more fear than pain behind the sound, and her job was to close the wound, regardless of her horse's discomfort.

Lee's fingers moved as gracefully and as smoothly as those of an experienced surgeon. She took her time, setting each individual stitch equidistant from the one before and tightening each with an almost imperceptible motion of the wrist. Carlos fed the catgut to her, keeping it straight and free of tangles. When Lee had secured the final knot, Carlos cut off the excess suture material with his pocketknife. Lee then applied a thin coating of a dark, thick, stringy paste of petroleum gel, wrapped the area with several layers of gauze, and attached a wide canvas belt over the dressing.

Lee stood and faltered for a moment, her knees protesting the half hour she'd spent crouching. After she stood, Rafe released the twitch, and Clover pushed at him with her muzzle, negotiating for a treat.

"How about a half scoop of sweet feed for the patient?" Lee said with a smile.

Rafe grinned as if he were getting a treat, not the mare. "Yes, ma'am," he said, slipping out of the stall. "Comin' right up!"

Carlos grinned too. "Ees very good job, Lee," he said. "Clover weel be good as *nuevo*."

That evening, Lee's private place on the hill over-looking the Busted Thumb seemed to be an oasis. The day had cooled. The power of the sun, which for several months had kept the nighttime temperature almost as high as that of the day, had abated—a sure sign autumn was approaching. She left Dixie grazing in a lush patch of grass that had been spared much of the killing wrath of the sun because of the shade of a few shrubs and four stunted desert pines.

In the soft light of the sunset, the Busted Thumb looked like a child's toy farm. A pair of geldings argued briefly in a pasture below her, then danced apart, snorting and posturing, rearing as if ready to do battle. Lee grinned. She knew both horses well, and a fight between them was about as likely as a fistfight between a pair of nuns. In a matter of moments, the horses stood together, head to tail, shagging flies from each other's faces and pulling lazily at the grass, their disagreement forgotten.

A happy peace washed over Lee. She walked to where Dixie was grazing and stroked the mare's neck. She didn't mount up; she wasn't quite ready to leave yet. Instead, she sat, leaned back against a boulder, and replayed the entire conversation with Harley Botts. She doubted anything the man said was true, and his claim of friendship with Jonas sounded as absurd in the replay as it had that morning.

Still, she was committed to the race—to Ben Flood and to Jonas and to the honor of her farm. To have Jonas Dwyer's horse beat Slick in a fair race would be a quick disappointment, but a proud moment too, in a way. Both animals were superior, stronger, more intelligent, and faster than other horses. But to have Slick lose to a horse owned by Harley Botts was absolutely unacceptable.

She pictured Wade on Slick clambering up that rock-littered slope. Then she remembered when Wade had called on her after Jonas's death . . . and she felt a quick flash of embarrassment at how Wade's eyes had affected her. *Must have been my grief,* she thought. *And the light wasn't good in the parlor. Shadows could've caused what I thought I saw. I'd just gotten up from a nap when we'd talked.*

Suddenly, the day came back with almost stunning clarity. As her own words that day rang through her mind, the physical sensations returned momentarily as well. She felt the hot, solid knot in her throat and the slight dizziness she'd experienced. She remembered the words she'd said. *Ben, I don't want how Jonas died to become common knowledge just yet. Can you hold back the part about him being murdered? And Carlos—don't tell the men about it either—just tell them Jonas died . . .*

Lee shifted her mind to the conversation she'd had with Wade later that afternoon. She remembered what Wade had said to her. *I'm sorry about Mr. Dwyer. I didn't know him, but the boys say he was a fine man. I know you were good friends, and I just kinda wanted to say . . . well . . . I'm sorry he got killed . . .*

*I'm sorry he got killed.*

Lee felt as if she'd been punched in the stomach. Carlos's word was as good as, or better than, a legal contract. He'd told the men about Jonas's death, but he'd mentioned nothing about murder. And Ben's word was as good as Carlos's.

How could Wade have known Jonas had been killed? Lee took several deep breaths to calm herself. By the time she'd mounted Dixie and was on her way down the hill, she'd made her decision. Her instincts had always been good before, and she was sure they were now.

Wade Stuart was a figure in the ambush killing of Jonas. She just didn't know why.

She saw the light from the lantern hanging in Slick's stall as she approached the barn, walking Dixie. She handed the reins to one of the men and asked that he put the mare in her stall and give her a bucket of fresh water. Then she entered the barn.

Wade was brushing Slick in the stall. His saddle was draped over the closed gate, a stirrup on each side. The familiar aroma of neat's-foot oil hung in the still air, and the fenders, cantle, seat, and fork looked freshly treated, glistening slightly in the lantern light. She watched him for a few moments before speaking.

"Mr. Stuart," she said, "I want you off Busted Thumb property immediately—which means right now. Get your horse and gather up your things and ride out of here. And never set foot on my property again."

Wade turned to her, his facing showing confusion and surprise. "Miss Morgan, what are you talking about? Why should I leave? I've got Slick in better condition than he's ever been in, and I've—"

"I'm not going to debate this with you," Lee interrupted. "Do as I said, and do it now."

Wade's eyes were slitted now, and a choleric red was creeping into his face. "I got pay coming to me, and I deserve to hear a reason for this," he said. The words were quiet, but the same sort of quiet that precedes a storm.

"I'll figure your pay to date and have one of the men bring it to Burnt Rock tomorrow. You can pick it up from Marshall Flood. Maybe then you'll take the opportunity to tell him how you knew Jonas was killed, rather than simply dying of natural causes."

Wade's laugh was like the snarl of an animal. "I don't know what you're talking about. And I'll tell you this, Miss Rich Lady Ranch Owner—I'm sick of your stupid rules and your religious ways and how you slide around in the barns all day like you were a man, giving orders and checking up on me."

He moved to his saddle and untied the slicker. After taking out his gun belt and pistol, he tossed the slicker aside. Then he buckled on the belt and tied down the holster before he stood straight and spoke to Lee again.

"You're not nearly as smart as you think you are," he said. "Seems like you missed a big point here: Who's gonna ride Slick in the race? You expect to find someone who's as good as I am before the Harvest Festival? If you do, you're plumb crazy. Ain't nobody within a thousand miles who can ride like I can, and you know it." He laughed. "Maybe you're gonna put your fat Mex pal on Slick—I'd pay good money to see that. Tell me who's gonna be on Slick's back that day, and then I'll think about leaving."

Lee struggled to keep her voice even. "You greatly overvalue yourself, Mr. Stuart. Greatly. Who rides my horse in that race is none of your business. I want you out of here and off the Busted Thumb right now. If you don't go, I'll send for the marshall."

"Flood?" Wade sneered. "He's an old man who's living on a rep he got twenty years ago, when he was still worth somethin'. What's he gonna do? Throw his Bible at me?" Wade opened the gate to Slick's stall, stepped out, and then lifted his saddle. He started out of the barn but turned back to face Lee. "You might better stick with women's stuff. You play in a man's world, you're gonna get hurt."

"Thanks for the advice," Lee answered curtly. "Now get off my ranch."

A quick crackle of hatred appeared in Wade's eyes and then disappeared. This time, Lee knew she hadn't imagined it.

The moon was huge in a cloudless sky as Lee stood at her kitchen window, watching Wade ride out of her line of vision. The kettle of water on the stove began to boil, and she busied herself preparing a cup of tea. Carlos and Maria had ordered her a pound tin of Earl Grey, her favorite, for Christmas last year. She used it sparingly; the tin was still half full. After the leaves had steeped, she sat at the table and sipped slowly, hoping that the calming properties of the tea would soothe her mind as it generally did.

As soon as her cup was empty, however, she was up and pacing the room. *Had Wade threatened me, or were his words just the talk of a bitter man? Will he try to make trouble in Burnt Rock or take out his venom on the Busted Thumb's buildings, horses—or people? Is he a danger to Ben?*

Lee chided herself for using Ben's name as a scare tactic to get Wade moving. Was Wade angry or crazy enough to pick a fight? She didn't know the answer to that question, but she remembered the undiluted hate in his eyes and shivered.

After a while, her mindless pacing began to grate on her nerves, so she sat at the table again, lightly fingering her empty teacup. Then, with a sigh, she carried the lantern to her office and opened the payroll ledger. She figured Wade Stuart's wages to that day, checked her figures, and then worked the combination to the small safe that rested next to her desk. The steel box wasn't much larger than a small packing crate, but it had taken five strong men to haul it from the freight wagon into the house. Carlos had built a support directly under it, in the storm cellar, to keep it from going through the floor.

Lee closed the door of the safe, as always enjoying the secure sound of the well-lubricated "snicksnicksnicksnick" as she spun the combination dial. She placed the bills into an envelope, which she then folded and put into her culottes pocket. After writing a quick note for Carlos, she took the lantern and went to her bedroom to fetch her 30.06, then headed outside.

The barn was filled with the late-night calm that somehow always appears where well-fed and well-cared-for animals sleep. Lee carried the lantern to the tack room, stopping just inside to breathe in the aroma of leather and wood and neat's-foot oil. She slid her rifle into a leather scabbard and tied it behind the cantle of her saddle, lacing the opening of the scabbard securely. She then hefted the saddle and went back out into the barn to select a horse.

Carlos and his men had been checking and trimming hooves that day, so there were several good geldings and mares available for the ride to Burnt Rock. Lee had decided on a lanky paint gelding she'd ridden several times before, when she noticed the lantern light reflecting in Slick's eyes as he stood at his stall gate. If he hadn't nickered a greeting, she'd probably have taken the paint.

Slick huffed and shifted about as Lee swung her blanket and saddle onto his back. When he nudged at her with his snout, she spoke sharply to him, and he settled down a bit. Patience was something Slick had never had. He'd no doubt been worked hard that day, yet he couldn't wait to be out again, stretching his muscles for the pure joy of doing so. Lee scratched the stallion's neck for a moment, then let her hand slide to the teak-hard muscle of his shoulder.

The rich scent of fresh-cut hay the crew had put up that day perfumed the air. Lee mounted the horse and eased him into a quick canter. By the time she turned in the saddle to look back over her shoulder, the Busted Thumb had disappeared. She and Slick were alone on a landscape softly lighted by the moon and countless stars like diamonds gently scattered on black velvet.

Lee could tell that Slick wanted to run. So did she, for that matter. She wanted to experience the exhilaration of his power and his speed. But she knew horses too well to allow the horse much more than a lope. The moonlight was as good at concealment as it was at illumination. Just as it revealed one prairie dog hole, it hid another in an inky shadow. Slick sulked a bit, much like a child commanded not to splash in a mud puddle, but he eventually resigned himself to the pace Lee demanded. Still, he shook his head every so often.

As she approached Burnt Rock, the only lights showing on the main sweep of the town were those of the Drovers' Inn and the marshall's office. She stayed on the dark side of the street as she rode past the saloon, but even then the stink of tobacco smoke and beer and the coarse, drunken shouts and baying laughter assaulted her like a foul wave from a stagnant sinkhole. When a gunshot sounded, Lee tightened her grip on the reins, waiting for Slick to bolt—or at least flinch in fear. He did neither, and for a moment she wondered at his lack of reaction. To the best of her knowledge, he had never heard the sound of a rifle or pistol shot.

The door to Ben's office was locked, a situation Lee had never encountered before. She knocked and heard the bolt being slid on the other side of the door.

"Lee!" Ben exclaimed.

She put her hand on Ben's forearm. "It's nothing, Ben—I'm all right. There's no big problem."

"Then what . . . ?"

Lee glanced over at Ben's desk and the visitor's chair in front of it. "Can we sit? I've had a long ride."

Ben looked over her shoulder at Slick standing at the hitching rail. He grinned. " 'Course, you didn't take any pleasure in the ride, did you?"

"Oh, hush, you," she laughed.

When they were seated and had cups of Ben's barely palatable coffee in front of them, he asked, "Why are you here?"

Lee nodded toward her cup. "I sure didn't ride here for that," she said. "You need to learn to make a pot of coffee that doesn't taste like cactus pulp, Ben."

"Maybe I need a lady to make coffee for me," he answered, looking up at her. She met his gaze, and neither spoke for what turned into an uncomfortably long time.

"Maybe you do," she said quietly, barely above a whisper, and then broke eye contact. She picked up her cup, sipped, and grimaced. When she spoke again, her voice was all business.

"I fired Wade Stuart earlier tonight. He didn't much like it. I told him he could pick up the pay I owed him here. I'm sorry I dragged you into the middle, but I thought . . ."

"You did the right thing. Don't apologize." He waited a moment and then asked, "Why'd you fire him? You've told me he's a good hand with horses and that he's conditioned Slick perfectly."

"Well, it was something he said right after Jonas was killed. Remember that I asked you and Carlos not to say anything about the way Jonas died?"

Ben nodded.

"Well, later that day, Wade stopped at my house to offer condolences. Ben—he used the words 'I'm sorry he got killed.' But he had no way of knowing how Jonas died. Jonas could've died from an illness, for all he knew."

Ben whooshed out a breath of air. For several moments, he was silent. "Stuart could have thought an accident of some kind took Jonas. Horse ranches can be dangerous places." When Lee began to speak, he held up his hand. "Wait—I'm not questioning your feelings here. I don't like what he said. I'm going to need to talk with him."

"Thanks. If you're not satisfied, can you arrest him?"

"That depends. Was there anyone else there? Maria? Carlos?"

Lee shook her head. "We were in my parlor, alone."

Ben leaned back in his chair. "Way back when you first hired Stuart, you had some bad feelings about him. I wired to the jurisdictions around here, askin' if any of the lawmen knew of Stuart or had even heard about him. I came up empty, but that means next to nothin'."

146

Lee shook her head. "Maybe I should have let him go after that blowup with Rafe. I wish I had."

"*Maybe* is a great big word, Lee. You had no way of knowin' about any of this back then."

"I guess. But I feel like I've dropped a kettle of trouble in your lap. If Wade turns out to be a gunfighter, he may—"

Ben reached across the desk and took her hand. He smiled, but his face was grim. "If it wasn't for kettles of trouble in my lap, I wouldn't have anything to do. I'm a marshall, remember?"

"I know that." She met his eyes. "And I didn't mean to imply that you can't do your job if it comes to locking up Wade. It's just that I hate to be the cause of putting you in danger."

She suddenly became aware of the fact that Ben was still holding her hand. She pulled away.

Ben cleared his throat. "The Harvest Days Festival is comin' up," he said. "Have you gotten a rider for Slick yet?"

"I may have—I'm not quite sure yet. Harley Botts came to talk to me yesterday with some ridiculous story about his being a close friend of Jonas, and how Jonas wanted him to have Pirate. It was lies. All of it. Botts is a snake, and I'm sure that Wade is somehow involved with him."

Ben nodded. "That thought crossed my mind too. Botts could have killed—or had somebody else kill—Jonas and then made some sort of a deal with Stuart about the race. Knowing the winner would mean a lot of money to someone crooked enough to set it all up."

"It could have been planned out ever since the race was first announced," Lee said. "Wade could've been playing me for a fool. Everyone here in town and for miles around knows what a great job he's done in bringing Slick into top form. There'll be lots of money bet on him to beat Pirate. All Wade would have to do is make the race look good, but let Pirate win. Botts would clean up—and so would Wade."

"That's why you need to find a man who can run that race on Slick to beat Pirate fair and square."

"I've pretty much made up my mind about that. And Slick *will* beat Pirate."

"Who is this rider, then? One of your men from the ranch?"

Lee smiled and sipped at the dregs of her coffee before answering. "Did I say anything about a man?"

# 9

Lee was alert and awake when she jogged Slick toward the barn on the Busted Thumb. Although she'd ridden most of the night, what she'd revealed to Ben had lifted her spirits and made her plan seem less harebrained and more real.

Of course, it wasn't a woman's place to ride a stud horse in a twenty-mile race. That was a man's place— and she knew she'd be accused of impropriety, even by the women of Burnt Rock. She remembered what a bank attorney had said when she'd requested a loan for the purchase of a dozen stallions: *It simply isn't done, madam.* She'd heard the same phrase when she purchased the Busted Thumb, began her breeding program, started gelding stallions not to be used for breeding, and ran her operation as she thought it should be run.

She smiled. She'd never told anyone, but she always felt a surge of excitement, a sort of tingle, when she broke the stuffy rules of the society around her. She didn't really consider herself rebellious, but there was a bit of . . . well . . . fun in thumbing her nose at the nonsense that strove to keep women in their "proper" place.

Perhaps it simply wasn't done—but she was going to do it. She was going to ride Slick in the contest, and she was going to win.

When Lee entered the barn, she saw Carlos sitting on a bale of fresh hay he'd placed outside Slick's stall. He was sipping at a mug of coffee. "I could 'ave ridden to town," he greeted her. "Such a ride at night by a woman alone ees *muy loco*."

"I needed to talk to Ben," Lee said. "And if I ran into trouble, who could catch me on Slick?"

Carlos didn't respond to her smile. "A prairie dog hole heeden in a shadow could catch you. A bullet fired by one of the scum who are filling up Burnt Rock could catch you, no?"

"It was important, Carlos—and I was perfectly safe. You worry about me too much." She added more softly, "And I appreciate it."

Carlos exaggerated a sigh of resignation. "Tell me," he said, "what wass so *importante* that it couldn't wait for the sun?"

It didn't take more than a few moments to fill in Carlos on her conversation with Wade, her firing of him, and the importance of giving Ben some advance notice on what could be a dangerous situation. As Carlos listened carefully, his posture changed. His mouth tightened and his face rose in color.

"You believe then that Wade an' thees other snake—Botts—had much to do with Jonas's death?"

"I believe that, yes. I do."

150

"I weel instruct the men to carry guns. I know your feelings about that, but we need to be careful—we need to protect ourselves an' our horses."

"Carlos—"

"You know thees ees true. *Por favor*—don' order me to no arm the men."

Lee thought for a moment. One person had already been murdered, and the men were very vulnerable if they weren't armed.

"You're right, Carlos. And I want Slick kept inside from now on. He'll miss his pasture time, but I'll be working him daily."

"Of course you weel," he said, a smile showing the whiteness of his teeth.

"What do you mean by 'of course'?"

Carlos's smile grew broader. "You thin' I'm a silly ol' man who don' know how your mind works after all our years? That I can't add two an' two together an' get four? You'll ride Slick in the race, no?"

Lee laughed. "Am I that easy to read?"

"As soon as you tol' me you fired Wade, I could see you running Slick at the Harvest Festival. You weel win. I know thees."

Lee laughed again. "All we need to do is convince everyone else that a lady riding in a race isn't a heretic or a witch, and we'll do fine."

Lee entered the barn with the first light the next morning, stopping in front of the man Carlos had posted to keep watch over Slick. She nudged his shoulder lightly, and his raucous snoring halted as if the sound had been cut off with a knife. He leaped to his feet, forgetting the rifle he'd rested across his lap.

"Miss Morgan! I was . . . just kinda . . ."

"You were sleeping is what you were doing, Jesse."

The young man kept his eyes on the floor. "Yeah. I was sleepin'. But, see, I'd worked on that string of fence near the front pasture all day yesterday an' was wore out some. That ain't light work, Miss Morgan."

"Why didn't you tell Carlos you were too tired to take the night watch without dozing off? There's no disgrace in that."

The man raised his eyes and looked at Lee. "'Cause I asked for this job. Slick, he's a right fine horse—best I ever seen. I was proud to be lookin' out for him. I was sure I could stay awake. Guess I was wrong."

"It's an important job."

"I know it is. Real important. Now you're gonna get one of the other men, an' I—"

"No, I'm not, Jesse," Lee said. "I want this to be your job until all the danger is gone and things get back to normal. You'll sleep during the day. And you'll stay awake at night, right?" She softened her words with a small smile.

"I sure will, Miss Morgan. I give you my word on that!"

"Tell Carlos what I've said as soon as you see him, and then get some sleep."

"You betcha! An' don't you worry none 'bout Slick at night!"

As Jesse hurried out of the barn, Lee shook her head silently and then chastised herself for doing so. Jesse was a good and loyal employee, and he was devoted to Slick's well-being. *What more could I ask of a guard?* she thought.

She continued deeper into the barn. Slick had been moved from his easily accessible front stall to a stall farther back in the building. He was standing to the rear of his windowless space, which wasn't like him at all. He'd always been a gregarious horse, hanging his head out into the aisle to watch whatever was going on or to greet whoever approached. It was rare that a worker or visitor would pass his stall without scratching his muzzle or stroking his neck. And Slick reveled in the attention.

But he didn't greet Lee; in fact, he barely looked at her.

His posture spoke as loudly as his apathy did. His head hung far lower than normal, and there was a laxness to his spine and stance. He appeared to be very, very tired, or perhaps even ill, although Lee was sure neither was the case. She sighed and stepped into the stall, attaching a lead rope to his halter. She saw that although he had drunk most of his water, his grain and molasses combination had barely been touched. The flake of hay tossed to him the night before hadn't been disturbed either.

She walked Slick up and down the length of the barn twice, checking for any sign of discomfort or pain in his legs and hooves. She listened carefully to his breathing and pressed her palm against his chest to check for a rapid heartbeat. As she suspected, there was no discernible physical problem with the stallion. The difficulty with Slick wasn't with his muscles or his nerves— it was with his heart. The bond he'd shared with Wade had been severed, and the horse was mourning the loss.

As Lee saddled Slick, Carlos walked into the barn. He stopped and looked at Slick for a moment, then shook his head. "You mus' ween heem back," he said. "Thees horse ees too smart to forget a friend. He stands here like a mule in front of a plow, no like the horse he ees."

"I know. Look at his eyes. It's like he no longer lives inside this body."

153

"There's but one way to bring heem back. Can you afford the time?"

"I'll find the time." She stroked Slick's neck. "Please have one of the men set up that old army cot for me. I'll sleep in the stall with Slick for a few nights and then move the cot right outside it."

Carlos nodded. "I'll tell the others that no one ees to feed or water heem or even muck out hees stall."

"Good. I'll get my bookwork done as I can and do all my other work from his back."

"You mus' keep in mind that as smart as he ees, he ees a horse. You will capture his heart queekly. Thees I know. Then Slick weel be back." He smiled. "Ees it such a terrible theeng to spend all your time with such a *grande* horse?"

"I'm looking forward to it."

"Maybe in your heart you were a leetle jealous of Wade?" Carlos asked.

Lee considered this for a moment and then felt her face flush. "Well . . ."

Carlos laughed.

Slick worked smoothly as Lee took him through his exercises, and he responded to cues and commands like the finely trained horse he was. But there was a difference that even a novice rider could notice. Slick didn't ask to run, and his stride at the gallop was shorter. He ran when Lee asked him to, but his fire was gone. And when Lee checked him after a mile at a gallop, he dropped back to a lope without argument. His stride was clean and even, but it was no longer the go-all-day pace he'd shown all his life.

Lee refused to allow her horse's mood to influence her own; that wouldn't do either of them any good. She

154

chatted at Slick, keeping a high pitch to her voice. She praised him lavishly, even when his performance was lackadaisical. And when she returned him to his stall a half dozen hours later, she broke one of her own rules: She treated him to a couple of chunks of sugar from her sugar bowl. This was a gift Slick couldn't refuse, but as soon as he'd swallowed, his head lowered and he looked away from her.

Later that night as she entered the barn, she decided that there were many worse places to sleep. The army cot was as unyielding as a block of marble, and sleeping in her clothes took some getting used to, but all her senses were in tune with the atmosphere. The aroma of the fresh straw and the clean scent of Slick's brushed coat, the sounds of the barn, the small movements of sleeping horses carried Lee back to her uncle's ranch in Virginia. She'd always felt very grown-up when she'd spent the night in a stall with a pregnant mare or an injured and frightened foal. She remembered one almost-due mare that had awakened her several times with the sensation of light, warm breath on her cheek. Lee wondered now who had been looking after whom.

When Lee awoke in Slick's stall the next morning, that thought was in her mind. Had Slick checked on her during the night? Had he brought his muzzle close to her? Or was she just dreaming? She had no way of knowing.

Carlos brought coffee and two warm rolls slathered with sweet butter and honey to Lee before the sun had chased away the darkness. Together they sipped coffee and ate their rolls in a companionable silence, listening to the barn awakening. An impatient mare whinnied, and another horse answered her. Carlos wiped crumbs from his mouth with his sleeve and said quietly, "Sometimes a man, he wonders."

155

"Hmmm?"

"What good ees money an' property an' power when we 'ave thees?"

Lee felt a quick tug at her heart. "You're a good man, Carlos," she said.

Carlos grunted, and Lee grinned at his embarrassment.

"After you ride, I'll work over Slick with the brushes an' you can wash up," he said, as much to draw attention from himself, she suspected, as to convey information. "You weel eat with Maria an' me at lunch an' supper?"

"I'd love to. After lunch I want to check on the mares in the south pasture."

Carlos laughed quietly.

"What? What are you laughing at?"

"Seems strange that anything you do on Slick is always as far away as possible, an' takes the longest ride. No?"

That morning Slick performed as he had the day before—almost flawlessly but with no more life or enthusiasm than a pack animal doing his job. Lee ran him in large figure eights on a half-acre flat atop a low rise, checking his leads and the flying change required at the center of each eight. Slick took his cues and was as smooth as the mechanism of a fine watch—and every bit as indifferent. Lee praised him for an exercise he'd mastered as a yearling, almost without training, but the horse didn't acknowledge his rider's pleasure.

The next several days passed with a depressing monotony, at least in terms of Slick's progress. Even though Lee's heart went out to her horse, frustration clutched at her each time he offered nothing but a sulking, halfhearted performance. He'd begun eating again

156

and didn't appear to have dropped any weight. Still, he was a stranger to Lee—an animal she didn't know and couldn't quite understand. She twisted about on the army cot at night, wondering if Slick really possessed the blood she wanted to help establish her ranch horse breed. Cowboys come and go on most cattle operations, she knew, but the horses stayed. Would Slick's progeny pine over each saddle tramp who worked a few seasons and then drifted on to the next place?

When Lee returned to the Busted Thumb after yet another disappointing few hours on Slick, Ben's horse, Snorty, was tied to the hitching rail at her house. She reined over to Carlos and Maria's home and found Ben and Carlos drinking coffee on the small porch. Ben waved and walked out to her as she swung down from Slick's back. As he approached, she noticed how haggard he looked—dark sacs hung under his eyes and his face was more angular than she'd ever seen it.

"Good to see you," she said. "What brings you out here?"

"This time it's good news, Lee—good news and the fact that I had to get out of Burnt Rock for a few hours."

She looked into her friend's eyes. "Are you getting *any* sleep? Are you eating?"

Ben's smile looked forced. "I've been sleepin' during the day. Nights have been busy. And I'm eatin' just fine. Bessie's been bringin' down meals to my office."

"Can you stay for dinner? We'd love to have you."

Maria peeked out from the front door. "I already asked heem, Lee. He says he don' like my cooking."

This brought a laugh from the marshall. "I said no such thing, Maria! I said I'd love to, but I need to get back."

"An' deal weeth creeminals 'stead of sitting weeth us? Card players an' gunmen are better than your friends at the Busted Thumb?"

"Not by a long shot," Ben answered. "Another time I'll stay."

"Ahhh, Ben," Maria said. "You know you're always welcome, no? I worry about you, *mi amigo*." She drew back behind the door before Ben could tell her there was nothing to worry about.

Carlos stood. "I'll see you before you ride out. I 'ave a foal to tend to right now."

"Good, Carlos," Ben said, then turned to Lee. "Let's put Slick in his stall. I want to give you the good news too." He took a yellow telegram from his pocket and handed it to her as they started to the barn. Snorty called out a challenge to Slick that brought Slick's head up quickly, as if to respond, but then he dropped it again.

When they reached the barn, Lee read the page.

```
Miss Lee Morgan
Busted Thumb Horse Ranch
Burnt Rock, Texas
C/O: Marshall Benjamin Flood

(Start) Dearest Lee:
    Thank you for wire concerning
Father's death and for Mr. Uriah Daily
(Stop) Did not know how bad Mother has
become (Stop) Father did not tell us
(Stop) Decided to come to Texas and take
over ranch (Stop) I arrive within three
weeks (Stop) Basil to arrive later
(Stop) I hope to arrive for Harvest
Festival and stay two days in town
(Stop) You are in our prayers (Stop)
    Janice Dwyer Taggart (End)
```

"Oh, Ben, this is wonderful!" Lee exclaimed. "Did you read this?"

He grinned. "I'm a marshall, not an angel. Of course I did. Maybe havin' Janice there will make a difference for Margaret. It's great news."

"Janice was always the brightest of the Dwyer kids. And her husband is a merchant of some kind and apparently knows business. They'll be good for Jonas's ranch."

"I hope she keeps ol' Verge on as manager," Ben said. "He's a good man, and he knows horses and how to keep them. From what I've heard, the hands at Dwyer like him and work well for him."

"I'm sure she will. I'll write out a wire to her before you leave, if you would be so kind to drop it at the telegraph office. I'll mention Vergil in it." She smiled. "Thank God for this, Ben. Jonas's people belong on that ranch."

She began stripping the saddle from Slick and roughing up his coat with a piece of burlap. Ben brushed some grit from Slick's chest.

"Carlos says you're having some trouble with this boy."

"Yeah. He's like a different animal since Wade left."

"Speaking of Wade," Ben said. "He stopped by to pick up his pay."

"And?"

"And nothing. He came in, walked to my desk, and held out his hand. I gave him his money, and he left. That was it."

Lee sighed. "Well . . . at least that's finished and over with, then. Do you know if he left town?"

"Not according to what Zach told me. He's been drinkin' up a storm at the Drovers'." Ben changed the subject quickly. "I had an idea about Slick that I mentioned to Carlos when we were talking."

"Oh?"

"Yeah. Back before the war, a friend of mine had a great running horse, and his trainer quit on him. The horse acted exactly like Slick is actin' now. My friend hired on a new trainer—a good one—and what this fellow did snapped the horse right out of his mood."

Lee stopped rubbing Slick and turned to Ben. "What did he do?"

"Well, he set up a race between that horse and another. The second was a good horse but didn't have the speed of the first. This was a flat race—maybe two or three miles is all. The thing is, the trainer riding the better horse held him in and let the other get a length on him. Then he went a mile or so with the good horse eatin' dust. Pretty soon the good horse was just about comin' apart, fightin' the bit and tossin' his head, dyin' to ram past the horse ahead of him. 'Course, the trainer finally threw that horse all the rein he wanted, and the race was over—the running horse pulled ahead in a heartbeat and beat the other by twenty-five lengths. My friend said his running horse started the race as one animal and finished it another."

"Of course!" Lee cried. "Any horse with heart resents being bested in a race. Maybe a simple thing like getting ahead of and beating another horse can shift Slick's mood."

"Here's the thing, though, Lee. My friend said that if the horse being taunted doesn't show enough heart to fight for his head, he's probably never gonna come around. He's lost his fire already, and if a race with another horse doesn't pull him out of himself, nothing will. His bottom would be gone."

Lee exhaled through pursed lips.

"I was told it's the smart ones, the clever, curious horses, that are the hardest on themselves and the hardest to bring back. This boy," he said, gesturing toward Slick, "is one of those. If he doesn't really want to win, he won't try to break away. And you'll be in bigger trouble than you're in now."

Less than an hour later, Ben headed back to town with a message for the Burnt Rock telegrapher in his pocket as Lee and Carlos stood together outside Slick's stall.

"Lucky's the one we use, I thin'," Carlos said. "He's a strong horse an' has some speed."

"But those two were at each other in the paddock a couple of weeks ago. There's some bad blood between—" Lee stopped herself as the idea caught her. She smiled.

"'Zactly," Carlos said with a grin. "Already, they don' like each other. We run jus' before dinner, no?"

Several hours later, Slick followed Lee out of the main barn, saddled and bridled—and apathetic. In front of the smaller breeding barn, Carlos pulled the cinch on Lucky's saddle. Lee grinned. Lucky was a handsome stallion, and, of course, he realized it. He stood 15.3 hands, and his coat was a flashy mix of blood-bay body, four white stockings, a white star on his forehead, and a broad white bib over his chest. His tail was full and luxurious, as was his mane, and both were almost black.

Lucky caught Slick's scent immediately and snorted a challenge. Slick looked toward Lucky for a moment and then looked away without responding. Carlos and Lucky set off at a walk, heading toward a long, semi-flat series of acres beyond the Busted Thumb's south pasture.

161

The day had started out hot and still, but by midafternoon a cooling breeze had arrived, lowering the temperature and chasing away the humidity. The sun remained high over the western horizon; it wouldn't be dark for a few more hours.

Lee held Slick back fifty feet behind Lucky, although there was little real holding to do. Slick walked as Lee instructed him to and seemed content with that pace. Lucky, however, spun to face Slick several times, trumpeting challenges.

Lee scratched Slick's neck, noticing that there was little tension in his muscles. Lucky and his taunts were only a minor distraction, if that. She sighed heavily. This race had seemed like a good idea, but now she wasn't so sure. If Slick didn't come alive against Lucky, maybe he never would. He'd be the sort of horse the West was full of: solid and dependable but listless, with the personality of a fence post. She'd have to geld him before she sold him, and that thought brought quick tears to her eyes.

Carlos eased Lucky into a lope. Lee gave enough rein for Slick to follow suit if he cared to. He maintained his walk until she asked for a lope with the pressure of her legs.

Carlos reined in, and Lee rode behind him and drew rein another ten feet to his side. Lucky tried to rear, snorting explosively, dancing in place as Carlos held him. Slick sidestepped away from Lucky's antics and kept a watchful eye on him afterward.

"Geeve me a good thirty or forty feet from the start. I'll let Lucky stretch, and then we see what happens. Ees OK?"

Lee waved at her friend. She didn't quite trust her voice.

162

"On *tres*?"

She waved again and tightened her hold on Slick. At the same time, she cued him to get under himself, to tighten his muscles and to place his hooves solidly for the launch forward. He responded sluggishly. Nevertheless, Lee could feel the tension flooding his muscles.

"*Uno . . . dos . . .*"

Lee used her boot heels lightly against Slick's sides while still holding him stationary.

"*TRES!*"

Lucky cannonballed forward and was in a full gallop within twenty feet. As he stretched his stride, the power of his legs dug lumps of dirt from the ground.

Slick's head snapped up as Lucky began to run. For a split second, nothing happened. Lee held Slick even tighter, then contradicted that order by tapping him with her heels and leaning forward in the saddle. She saw the change in the muscles of his neck; they suddenly hardened into thick cords. His body trembled as if with a fever, and a moan turned into the frustrated roar of a caged mountain cat, full of defiance and fury.

Lee let Slick go. His initial charge was so abrupt and so powerful that he almost left her behind. Grabbing a handful of mane, she struggled to regain her seat. Then she whooped with joy, shrieking her exhilaration to Slick, to Carlos, to Lucky, and to the prairie.

There was no contest.

Slick reached ahead for turf in a stretch longer than Lee had ever seen him accomplish. Suddenly, he was next to Lucky, his teeth bared in a snarl, frantic to tear a mouthful of hide from the silly upstart who'd dared to challenge him. The only way Lee could spare Lucky a painful wound was to jerk Slick's head away, and that's what she did.

She whooped again and heard Carlos whoop behind her.

The ride back to the Busted Thumb consisted of Slick's shenanigans to reach Lucky, and Lucky's attempts to spin and bolt from him. Even on a tight rein and with stern commands from Lee, Slick danced in place, snapping his hooves up almost before they touched the ground.

Finally giving up, Lee let Slick run again, leaving Lucky and Carlos far behind. When she had reined down to a canter and was offering a prayer of gratitude, she heard a gunshot from the Busted Thumb. Again, she asked Slick to run, swinging him in a wide, easy arc toward home.

When she arrived, she saw three men on horseback facing Rafe at the front of the main barn. Holding a double-barreled shotgun across his chest, Rafe had his finger inside the trigger guard. Two other Busted Thumb men held pistols, and several more workers were running toward the group. Lee reined in Slick, handed him off to a ranch hand, and ran to the cluster of men at the barn.

They were gamblers or worse, Lee realized as she looked at the three on horseback. They were dressed as lawyers or bankers, in suits and starched shirts, and although their clothing was clean and well pressed, there was a seediness to them—hair oiled but too long unwashed, eyes weak and reddened, and posture slightly slump shouldered.

"What's going on here?" Lee demanded.

"Miss Lee," Rafe said, "these yahoos came ridin' in here, wantin' to see Slick. I tol' 'em we couldn't give no barn tours and they could see him at the Harvest—"

"Lady," the gambler in the middle interrupted, "you'd best git your husband out here to talk with us, or some of these farm boys ain't gonna see tomorra." He fingered his gun, which was still in the holster.

Carlos arrived just then and dragged Lucky to a sliding stop. Pistol in hand, he was off the horse in a moment and standing next to Lee.

The gambler laughed. "A pretty thing like you married up with a Mex? He musta had a ton of pesos to git a rope on a—"

Carlos fired once, and the gambler's face went white. A trickle of blood flowed from his temple and down his cheek, then dripped in coin-sized blotches on his white shirt.

"You thin' I miss? You're wrong. Next time I fire, you get a new eye. You understan'?"

"Lookit here," another of the trio said. "We ain't lookin' for no gunplay. That fool with the shotgun drew down on us soon's we rode in! All we want's a look at that horse Slick 'fore we bet on or agin' him. Ain't no crime in that, is there?"

"Get off my property," Lee said.

"Lookit here—" the man began again. When Carlos thumbed back the hammer of his Colt, the gambler shut up.

"You hear the lady, no? Ride back to where you come from. I see you on thees lan' again, an' I shoot to keel."

Almost in unison, the three men reined their horses around and started off, spurring their animals into a lope after they'd gone a few yards.

"Miss Lee," Rafe said after the men had ridden off, "I fired over their heads. They come bustin' in like they owned the Busted Thumb."

165

"You did the right thing," she assured him. "I'm sorry you had to, but I'm glad you did." She turned to the other hands. "I want you men to continue to be alert for scum like those three. Fire off a couple shots at the sky and don't let them near any of our horses, not just Slick. We'll all come running."

The men nodded their agreement and then drifted off, talking among themselves.

"One more week and this will all be over," Lee said to Carlos, who still stood beside her.

"It can no come soon enough. The men, they're ranch hands, not *pistoleros*. They're scared, Lee."

"You know something? So am I."

# 10

Janice Dwyer—now Janice Taggart—had been a quiet, introspective child. The brightest of the Dwyer youngsters, she'd spent most of her free time between the covers of a book. She liked horses—loved them, in fact—but was far more interested in them as creatures of their Creator than as drudges to be run hard or used for transportation

Janice remained childless after three years of marriage. She confided to Lee that she hoped that situation would change soon. She wanted very much to raise children where she herself had been raised.

Now, in the Merchant's Rest Hotel in Burnt Rock, where they shared a room with a pair of beds constructed with the newfangled springs rather than shuck material and wooden boards, Janice and Lee renewed their friendship.

Lee sat on a bed in the hotel room, trying to hold her nervousness at bay. She hated to be away from the Busted Thumb even for these two days. Slick was under twenty-four-hour armed guard at the livery stable on Main Street, but even so, she couldn't help but worry about his safety. She knew that she and Slick needed to be here the day before the race, but this didn't make her any less uncomfortable.

Lee flinched as another gunshot sounded along Main Street. Although the Merchant's Rest Hotel was at the opposite end of the street from the Drovers' Inn, the racket from the saloon sounded as if it were coming from next door.

Janice looked up from the Ned Buntline novel *Gunfighter's Trouble on Boot Hill* that had been left by the previous tenant of the room. "You need to relax," she said. "Nothing we can do is going to stop those men from being the louts and drunks they are, and you need sleep for tomorrow."

"I know," Lee sighed. "But I doubt I'll get much sleep tonight. I'm as nervous as a long-tailed cat in a roomful of rocking chairs."

Whoops, shouts, and the drumming of hooves interrupted the conversation. Lee moved to the window and watched three men on horseback blast past below, their mounts at full gallop. She looked as they passed the "Welcome to the Burnt Rock Harvest Days Festival" banner that was strung across the street—the same banner that would serve as the start/finish line tomorrow morning. The cloud of dust the trio of horses put in the air reached the second floor, and Lee lowered the window a bit.

"I'm going over to the livery stable to look in on Carlos and Rafe," she said.

"Give ol' Slick a kiss behind his ear for me," Janice replied. "Make him promise to win tomorrow." She paused. "Isn't that strange? I'm hoping another horse beats my father's prime stallion. Doesn't make much sense, does it?"

"It makes a lot of sense—because your dad doesn't own Pirate anymore. That good horse is owned by a thief, a gambler, and a liar."

"I know that. I just wish you weren't going to be riding tomorrow."

"We've been over this before," Lee said quietly.

"No, *we* haven't. You have! Every time I bring up the subject, you go on and on about what a tremendous rider you are, and how the race isn't dangerous, and a bushel of other nonsense!"

"Janice . . . please—"

"Don't *please* me, Lee Morgan! You're just being prideful and pigheaded about this whole thing!" She slammed her book shut. Then, after a long moment of strained silence, she said, "I'm afraid for you, Lee, out there on the prairie all alone."

"I won't be riding alone tomorrow," Lee said. "A power far greater than you or me will be with me."

After she gave Janice's shoulder a squeeze, Lee walked quickly from the hotel, her eyes sweeping the darkened streets. She chided herself for being nervous, but nevertheless, another gunshot caused her to jump as if she'd stepped on a snake. She felt immense relief when she approached the blacksmith shop and livery stable, which cast light from each of its windows into the darkness of Burnt Rock. The stable's interior was brighter than day. Five or six lanterns were needed to illuminate the inside of the stall and forge areas; ten were lit and turned up high.

Cradling a shotgun, Rafe was walking the periphery of the building. He waved to Lee but didn't slow his pace. Inside the barn, Carlos stood at the forge, a mug in his hand. The blacksmith's fire was down to red coals, and a kettle of coffee hung from the crosspiece.

"I no remember the coffeepot," Carlos said in greeting. "But thees kettle coffee is no so bad. You'll 'ave a mug?"

"No thanks. I've had a gallon at the café today. Everything quiet here?"

"As quiet as it weel get until after thees ees over. Slick ees used to his stall. Ees a good thing we brought heem here yesterday."

The nicker from Slick's stall brought a smile to Lee's face. She walked over to the horse. The window near him had been boarded over, but a lantern hanging from a rafter provided all the light she needed. She stroked his muzzle, looking deep into his eyes. Slick shifted, extending his neck over the stall gate a bit farther, nuzzling at Lee for a treat. She gently but firmly pushed his face away.

"What a mistake it was to give Slick that sugar! He's still looking for more," she called to Carlos.

"Maybe I gotta teach you somethin' 'bout horses, Lee. You let a smart one like thees get away with anything once, and he weel never let you forget it."

"I know," Lee said, laughing. She stepped into the stall, pulling the gate closed behind her. Then she stood at Slick's shoulder, facing in the opposite direction, and picked up his left front hoof.

She looked at the hoof, admiring the work of Angelo, the Burnt Rock blacksmith. He'd shod cavalry mounts and officers' horses throughout the war, once even shoeing General Grant's stallion. The new shoes he'd nailed onto Slick's hooves were fitted perfectly, and the clinches were tight, each precisely the same size as the others. The new steel glinted where Angelo's rasp had scraped away the surface metal. Lee went from hoof to hoof, inspecting each carefully.

"What do you think about contracting with Angelo to come to the ranch every few weeks to work on our best horses, Carlos?"

Carlos chuckled. "Ees no need," he said. "I already deed—every three weeks, no? To trim an' reset an' new shoes for those who need them. I'm very old to 'ave the horses sit on my shoulder while I try to feet them right."

"And too fat too," Lee observed, goading her friend.

"Ees all muscle. An' should I tell Maria, 'I can eat no more of what you made for me?' No. You tell her that an' she run you out of the house."

Lee left the stall and locked the gate. "Well, he looks beautiful," she said. "If I lose tomorrow, it won't be Slick's fault."

"You won' lose. Jus' remember—the race ees not won going out, ees won on the way back. You save Slick an' he'll bring you home ahead of Pirate. Thees I know."

"I'll do my best. I guess I'll have to run the race as I see it." She paused. "Any word on who's riding for Botts tomorrow?"

"Don' matter. I heard some boy who did some racing las' fall in the South. Like I say, it don' matter. You an' Slick, you weel win." His eyes held hers for a moment. "I'll go to Ben now, wearing thees." He pinned on the brass star of a deputy marshall that Ben had given him almost a year ago at another time when he'd needed a dependable man with him. "Ben says the oath is steel good." He grinned. "But I ride with Ben Flood, oath or no oath."

171

"Be careful, Carlos."

"An' you, my friend. You be careful too."

Janice was asleep when Lee returned to the hotel. Lee pulled a chair close to the open window and stared out into the night. The moon was almost full, but the sky was clogged with dark clouds. Snake tongues of lightning flickered in the distance, although she heard no thunder. And what breeze there had been earlier in the evening had died down; the Harvest Days banner hung limply, sagging toward its center.

The tinkling chords of Zach's piano at the Drovers' Inn reached Lee, as did bursts of strident laughter. With no wind to dissipate the noise, curse words were clear in the yells and shouts from the saloon. She lowered the window, then opened it again within ten minutes, surprised at how stifling the room had become in such a short time.

After she opened the window, she prayed for guidance and for the skill to ride Slick wisely. She prayed for the Lord to bring peace to Burnt Rock and to rest his hand on Ben Flood's shoulder as he faced the chaos that was sure to come the next day.

Wade Stuart stood next to the man on the piano bench, glaring at him, his arms folded across his chest. His eyes were reddened and crusty, and several days' growth of stubble darkened his face. His hat was gone, and his blond hair was knotted and greasy and lay against his skull as if glued there. His shirt stuck to the sweat on his back and chest, and both his shirt and pants held bits of sawdust from the floor in the Drovers' Inn.

Alcohol now controlled Wade—alcohol and hatred. In the past, he'd ride into a town, run a scam, and ride on with money in his pockets, perhaps with a fresh notch in the grip of his Colt. But now rage boiled.

He leaned closer to Zach. "I'm real sick of the junk you play," he snarled. "You don't know nothin' but that Union trash."

" 'When Johnny Comes Marching Home' is a Confederate tune," Zach protested, "and I just played that."

"Union crybaby junk's what it is—and don't you smart mouth me!" Wade let his hands drop to his sides. He touched the grips of his Colt with his right index finger, as if to assure himself that the weapon was right where it was supposed to be. "I want you to play 'Dixie,' and I want you to sing it too."

Zach stopped his playing and brought his hands to his lap. The silence from the piano didn't make a difference in the racket of the bar; the noise level hadn't changed at all. Zach turned his body on the piano bench to face Wade and spoke loud enough to be heard, and not a bit louder. "I won't do that. Make another request, please."

"You call me 'sir' when you speak to me!" Wade bellowed. His face was now red, and bits of dry spittle had gathered at the corners of his mouth.

"President Lincoln promised me a few years ago that I'd never have to call another man 'sir' unless I felt he deserved that designation. You don't." Zach turned back to his piano and fingered the beginning of a dance tune.

Wade drew his Colt and nudged the barrel into Zach's left ear. "Here's what you're gonna do: You're gonna play an' sing 'Dixie,' an' then you're gonna call me 'sir.' Understand that?" He drew back the hammer.

Zach swallowed hard, but when he spoke, his voice was clear and free of emotion. "All that was killed and buried twice already—once by Abe Lincoln and again at Appomattox."

Wade stumbled back a half step as if he'd been shoved by an invisible hand. His lips moved slightly, but no words were audible. Easing the hammer of his pistol down, he stood with the gun hanging loosely from his hand. The hot scent of potential violence and bloodshed caught the attention of the crowd. Heads in the saloon began to turn toward the two men.

In a heartbeat, the numbness left Wade's face, which became a twisted mask of loathing. His right hand struck out, smashing his pistol across the upper part of Zach's face. The grinding snap of cartilage in Zach's nose was as loud as the impact of the steel against flesh. He flew to the floor, blood gushing from both nostrils and from a deep cut above his right eye.

Dazed, he sat up and began to bring his hand to his face when Wade dragged him to his feet, turned him toward the front of the saloon, and shoved him hard. "Get outta here! Next time I see you, I'll kill you!"

Zach lumbered ahead a couple of steps, blinded by blood and barely conscious. Wade jammed his Colt into its holster and grabbed the back of a man's chair, hauling it out from under him and dropping him to the floor. He swung the chair for momentum and then threw it at the retreating Zach, missing him by a foot. The chair continued onward, exploding through the large front window facing Main Street.

Ben had his key in his hand and was fitting it to the lock on his office door when a chair struck the front window of the Drovers' Inn. Carlos, a step behind him, reacted just as he had: He began running toward the source of the sound. A moment later as Ben came into pistol range, Wade bulled through the batwings and stood on the wooden sidewalk, his hand hovering near the grips of his pistol.

"Don't do it, Stuart!" Ben bellowed.

Carlos stopped slightly behind and to the right of the lawman, his shotgun barrel sweeping over Wade and the other men who'd rushed out into the street after him.

Wade spread his boots a bit farther apart, facing Ben over the twenty feet that separated them.

"Don't even think about it," Ben said. "This doesn't have to go any further. Grab your horse and ride on. Burnt Rock has had enough of you."

The drunks and gamblers tripped over one another getting out of the line of fire, their eyes hot with anticipation of the gunfight. One gambler quickly offered even odds, and another upped that with two for one in favor of Wade.

"I'm not leaving, Flood. Your badge doesn't scare me, and your fancy girlfriend with her stinkin' ranch doesn't either. I'm better than you've ever been. You're gonna die here in the street, lawman."

Ben's mouth was dry. He swallowed to generate saliva before he spoke. "There's no reason for anyone to die over a bar fight. Get your horse and point him out of my town."

"You fought with the Union, didn't you, Flood? That's another real good reason for me to shoot you down like a cowardly dog."

"It doesn't matter who I fought with. The war is over. I'm not gonna tell you again what I want you to do."

"What you want me to do? I don't take orders from a yellowbellied Union soldier boy!"

Ben watched the slits of Wade's eyes. The light from inside the saloon put an eerie glint in the gunslinger's unblinking stare. Ben knew that a person's eyes would change the slightest bit the instant before he made his move. The time for talking was over.

Curving slightly inward, his fingertips touched the grip of his Colt as tenderly as a butterfly lands on a flower. Wade mirrored his stance.

"You're goin' down, Flood," he said, barely above a whisper. "And I'll tell you this before you die . . ."

It was an old trick, and often a deadly one in other towns and Western streets. Distract the opponent the smallest bit and then draw—put a bullet in the other man while he tried to absorb what was being said.

Ben's Colt cleared leather as Wade's hand slapped the grips of his weapon. The horse trainer's barrel was rising to spit death. Ben fired twice, the reports blurring together and sounding as one shot. The impact of the two slugs—one in the right shoulder, the other just above the elbow on the same side—hurled Wade back against the frame of the batwing doors. His face showed first surprise and then flashed with hatred.

Amazingly, he hadn't lost his Colt. It hung limply from his right hand, blood from his wounds sluicing past it to pool on the dust and dried wood of the sidewalk.

Ben saw what was coming, but his mind refused to accept it. *No one in his right mind would try a border shuffle when he already has a gun trained on his heart!*

"Don't, Stuart!" Ben snapped. "Don't do—"

Wade launched his pistol toward his waiting left hand. It wasn't a perfect pass, but it worked. He squeezed the trigger as he raised the barrel, but two more slugs from Ben's Colt punched him in the chest before his own pistol fired the single round that hissed off into the darkness.

Wade, this time thrown directly at the batwings, crashed through the doors and into the saloon.

Carlos and Ben rushed in after him. Carlos roughly grabbed a gambler by the shoulder and shouted at him, "Get Doc—and be quick about it! I know your face—you don' bring Doc, then I come an' look for you, no?"

The man stumbled from his seat and hurried out of the room. After he left, the silence in the Drovers' Inn was thick and threatening. Ben could smell the metallic scent of fresh blood. He crouched next to Wade, placing his fingertips first at the man's throat and then at his wrist. There was no pulse. He stood and saw that Zach was sitting up near the door of the saloon. Carlos was hunkered down next to him.

"Carlos," Ben said, and nodded to the shotgun. Carlos tossed it to him. Ben turned and surveyed the saloon.

Botts and his men had two tables side by side at the back of the room, guarded by three or four others. A hand-lettered sign nailed to the wall behind the tables stated:

### 4 TO 1 FOR PIRATE
### BEST ODDS IN TOWN!!!

A metal strongbox the size of a suitcase was open in front of Botts, and it was filled with money and hand-written slips carrying names and amounts.

Ben waited a long moment before speaking. "This place is closed for the night. Everyone get out."

A murmur started and quickly became louder. Ben leveled the shotgun at the tiers of whiskey bottles behind the bar and pulled the trigger. The blast of the twelve-gauge in the confined space was like that of an artillery piece. The bits of shot tore through the bottles, filling the air first with shards and splinters of glass, then with the acrid stench of whiskey.

"Move," Ben said. "Now!"

Reluctantly, the Drovers' Inn emptied its collection of depravity into the street.

The children—busy with chasing one another around the booths and displays along Main Street—seemed to be the only ones who didn't look up at the leaden gray sky. It was the children too who were best at ignoring the stifling heaviness of the air and the temperature that was high enough to wet a man's shirt even if he was standing still.

The farmers were no doubt the first to notice the flickering of lightning to the north and west and the dark clouds beginning to roil and churn. Perpetual sky watchers, the farmers knew cloud formations and the taste of the air as well as they knew their own families—and if they were successful farmers, perhaps better. They noticed how the ownerless dogs of Burnt Rock were acting, and that bothered them as much as the sky.

The homeless dogs skulked around corners, tongues lolling as if cringing from a raised hand. They sought shelter rather than food scraps dropped by adults or treats offered by children. Those hiding under the bandstand had to be forcibly evicted when two of them began yowling at the music of an elderly flautist. She herself delivered a solid kick to the rear of one of the animals' scurrying hindquarters before continuing her number.

There were fewer tables offering cold sarsaparilla and lemonade this year; O'Keefe's Café not only didn't have a stand, but the restaurant itself was closed for the duration of the festival. Still, vendors strolled about, selling apples and hard candy and small American flags on sticks, and the scent of a roasting steer helped whet appetites.

Just as they did every year, the grizzled old buffalo hunters dominated the target shooting contest with their Sharp's rifles. There was some grumbling when the marshall cancelled the pistol contest, limiting the shooting to long guns only, but grumbling citizens were the very least of the lawman's problems.

The crowd was radically different from those of earlier Harvest Days Festivals in the town. Holstered pistols hung on the hips of the majority of the men, and there were several uniformed Union officers—horse buyers—generally older gentlemen with wide girths and polished boots.

Ben and Carlos seemed to be everywhere at once, and both showed the strain of a sleepless night. The knuckles on Carlos's right hand were abraded and bleeding as the result of a run-in with a belligerent drunk who didn't care to spend the day in jail, and the deputy's badge that was pinned to his shirt had a drop of dried blood on it. Ben's face was a hard mask, and his eyes moved rapidly over the people in the streets. He'd allowed the Drovers' Inn to reopen that morning solely because he believed the crowd of red-eyed gamblers and gunmen would cause less trouble inside the saloon than they would out on the streets.

Close to noon, people began assembling on the sides of Main Street, awaiting the start of the race. The gamblers, however, weren't interested in the start of the race; it was the finish that was important to them. They lined the bar and filled the tables in the Drovers' Inn. Only one of Botts's men was still taking bets, and he was doing very little business. Anyone wagering had already done so.

Lee stood in a shadow at the rear of the barn, her Stetson pulled low on her face and her eyes closed. Her hair was tucked into the collar of the chambray work shirt she wore. Her denim trousers were still stiff and felt like slabs of wood on her legs. She knew there'd be talk about the pants, but decided the talk was easier to disregard than the thorns and brambles she was liable to encounter.

Botts's rider, Juan, stood outside Pirate's stall, smoking a cigarette he'd just rolled. He was a short man—approximately five feet, three inches—and looked like he weighed less than a good bale of hay. His hair reached the middle of his back, and his face was narrow and tanned. A riding crop was attached to his right wrist with a leather thong, and the rowels of his spurs were made for punishment, not guidance. Lee immediately disliked him.

She stepped into the lantern light. Rafe stood in front of Slick's stall, his rifle cradled in his arms. She smiled at him, and he quickly but nervously returned a smile of his own. He didn't offer to help her as she saddled Slick, and for that she was glad.

Mounting in a barn was a greenhorn move, Lee knew. Nevertheless, she led Slick to a point twenty feet behind Pirate and Juan, who waited at the still-closed barn door, and swung into her saddle. Juan was already up, looking straight ahead, apparently staring at nothing.

The blacksmith slid the huge door along its track, and Juan rode out into the street. Lee gave him a few moments and then followed, keeping a tight rein on Slick. The stallion stopped just outside the barn door,

180

startled by all the people and smells and noise. He snorted and shook his head, but Lee easily quieted him.

She wondered how many of the townspeople recognized her in her cowhand gear. Her eyes found Carlos's grinning face halfway to the banner, and she managed a smile. Then her eyes rested on Ben, who was standing at the starting line, and for a moment they locked gazes.

The two stallions had ignored one another until they were brought close together, and then they began to assert themselves. Slick reached over for a bite of hide, and Pirate reared and snorted, wanting to strike back with his front hooves. Juan reined Pirate into a tight circle and held him in position. Lee settled Slick and held him in check. A whistling scream of challenge rose from deep in her horse's chest, and his muscles quivered under her, his neck as hard as marble with the tension.

Botts apparently knew better than to delay the start. He raised his pistol and bellowed, "On three! One . . . two . . ."

The sound of the .45 had barely punctuated the air when both horses launched themselves forward as if they'd been fired from a gigantic slingshot. Lee leaned low over Slick's neck, letting him stretch and grab the lead from Pirate.

The horses ran strong, carried by the awesome power of their legs, their shoulders, their every muscle. Lee allowed Slick his headlong gallop until she heard the receding pounding of Pirate's hoofbeats and was sure that Juan was at least six or eight lengths behind her. She argued Slick down to a fast lope and settled deeper into the saddle, watching the ground in front of her, afraid to take the time to glance over her shoulder to check on the competition. She didn't know this ground, and she didn't know where prairie dogs had decided to establish one of their towns.

It was then that the first cooling drops of rain began to fall, raising tiny puffs of dust where they struck the ground. A gentle, soothing mist washed the sweat from Lee's face. Smiling at the sweetness of the rain, she opened her mouth to it as a child does to a snowflake. She reached over to Slick's neck with her right hand and stroked it.

Suddenly her eyes were aflame. As an unearthly screech like that of all-powerful hands ripping apart a sheet of steel screamed in her ears, a tall saguaro cactus not thirty feet away exploded into shards of smoking shrapnel. The lightning had been so sudden and so violent that her eyes had no time to protect themselves with a blink.

Slick scrambled for his footing, intuitively more afraid of falling at high speed than he was of the monster that had attacked from the sky. Lee gave him the reins to let him find his balance, still seeing nothing but a brilliant white burst of intense light.

Just as quickly as he'd faltered, Slick recovered and was again running hard without command from his rider. Lee frantically rubbed at her eyes with the back of her hand. She felt rather than heard Pirate closing in on her; she could hear nothing but a piercingly painful whine like that of a lumber-mill saw. She turned her face up and forced her eyes open, letting the rain soothe them as best it could. Soon forms were beginning to take shape in front of her, but they were indistinct and glittery.

She had no choice. She dragged Slick to a hard stop and felt the earth tremble as Pirate and Juan galloped past her. Slick screamed his frustration, reared, attempted to get under himself to run again. The rain, which had picked up in intensity, cruelly slapped at Lee's face. She held Slick with the reins grasped in her right hand and sluiced water from her face and into her eyes with her left, ignoring the pain. Slowly, shapes began turning into objects. She saw a race trail marker—a blaze of red flaring from the top of a cactus a hundred yards ahead of her. Beyond that, she could see Pirate becoming smaller as he raced away.

She gave Slick all the rein he needed. She knew that if Pirate got any farther ahead, it might be impossible to catch him.

Slick halved the distance between himself and Pirate quickly and then halved it again. Lee's hearing was returning, and the first sound she was able to distinguish was the harshness of Slick's breathing. She slowed him to a fast lope and took a tight rein on him. As long as he could see Pirate ahead of him, he'd fight her, but she couldn't afford to use up her horse in the first part of the race. She gave Pirate his twenty yards and kept Slick at a steady pace, neither gaining nor losing ground on Juan.

The rain had become a wall of water that turned the prairie into soup and drove at the riders and horses like a living force. Thunder reverberated like drumbeats in the sky, and lightning streaked and branched in the churning clouds, skewering tall saguaros and reducing them to hissing globs of pulp.

Pirate disappeared from Lee's view as if he'd dropped into the earth—which, in fact, he had. Lee reacted too slowly; her mind told her what had happened, but her hands couldn't move fast enough. For a dizzying moment, she and her mount were airborne, and then they dropped eight feet to the several inches of water accumulating just

below the blind bluff that neither she nor Juan had anticipated. She whispered a prayer as she felt Slick collect
himself. They had slammed down hard, but the water
and the mud underneath had softened the jolt. Ten yards
ahead, what had probably once been a slow, shallow
stream was roaring like an enraged beast, frothing and
racing with itself.

Pirate was rearing and spinning, trying to dump Juan
and apparently wanting to get far away from the unfa-
miliar and frightening rush of water. As she and Slick
approached the torrent, Lee heard the sharp report of
Juan's quirt against Pirate's flanks. Slick bared his teeth
and again hurled his challenge at the other horse, and
Lee used his momentum and her heels to slide her
mount in a sloppy circle and out into the water. Slick
snorted, spooked by the rush against his legs, and then
did what Lee had hoped he would—he hurled himself
forward, fighting the strength of the current.

He barged out of the water at the far side, and Lee
stopped him, letting him breathe and drawing deep
breaths herself. She turned in the saddle and watched
as Juan flailed his crop against Pirate's sides. When the
panicked horse dragged his head around away from the
water, Lee gasped as Juan slashed the lash across Pirate's
muzzle again and again, forcing the stallion to face and
enter the water. Lee squinted into the rain and gasped
again when she saw the bright red on Pirate's side that
was quickly diluted by the downpour. Bile rose in her
throat. She screamed at Juan, not in words, but in an
almost primal fury that scorched her throat. She
watched Pirate begin the crossing, the whites of his eyes
seeming as large as dinner plates.

A mile ahead, an outcropping stood like a monolith
shrouded by shifting clouds and sheets of rain. She knew

there was nothing she could do for Pirate right now. She urged Slick toward the outcropping.

Holding Slick to a slow lope, she let him pick his own way through the muck that grabbed at his hooves with each stride. When she rounded the shoulder of the outcropping, she gave it lots of distance because she was concerned about stones and rocks that had rolled down to the prairie floor over the years. Then she stopped and stepped down from the saddle, holding a rein in one hand as she walked around Slick. She looked him over, touching his legs and pasterns and watching the pattern of his breathing. It was evident to her that he was tired. She gazed at the hill directly ahead of her. *If we can climb this side and make it down the other side without a wreck, I'd cut at least two or three miles from the ride. Maybe I'd be far enough ahead of Pirate that Juan would see he couldn't catch us, and he'd give up the contest.*

She didn't think he would try the climb. Anyone who'd quirt a horse's face couldn't ride well enough to make such an ascent. And the descent would be even more treacherous.

She stood directly in front of Slick. His eyes hadn't lost an iota of their fire. He was ready. Was she?

She closed her eyes and let the rain sweep over her for a minute as Slick nudged at her to get moving. After climbing into the saddle, she pointed Slick at the hill. She realized that she would be excess baggage on this part of the trip, so she gave all her rein to Slick and left the path to him. He'd proven his agility and his heart many times before, and she trusted him completely to do so now.

She flinched at the crack of Juan's whip against Pirate's hide. Behind her, she heard Pirate splashing through the mud. Slick picked his way upward, his nose close to the rocks and the sloppy, rushing mud that was cascading down the slope. He snorted nervously several times as he climbed, but he never halted. Lee knew that his instinct was telling him that if he stopped, he'd probably not be able to get started again. He needed his momentum, and he used it wisely.

Slick badly stumbled only once, going down on his front knees with his rear hooves digging for traction. Lee leaned back, giving Slick whatever benefit her slight weight could over his rear quarters. Long strands of spittle hung from his mouth, and his breath rasped in his chest as he dug himself out of trouble. As Slick freed himself, Lee took a breath, realizing she'd been holding it in almost to the point of dizziness.

The wind was stronger at the top of the outcropping, and the rain was driving harder. The thunder, now receding, continued to growl as Lee looked down at what seemed to be a straight-down incline a thousand miles long. Stepping stiff legged into the rocks and mire, Slick snorted and braced himself. He held his head high to counterbalance the slide his thirteen-hundred-pound body wanted to fall prey to.

Lee swallowed and then closed her eyes. It was up to the horse to get the both of them down—she knew she must leave the descent to him. Slick placed his hooves so rigidly that the impact traveled up his legs and into her body with each step. She welded her hands to the saddle horn as Slick scrambled down a face of flat rock.

Then, miraculously, they were at the bottom.

Slick's breathing was fast and labored, and he hung his head for a long moment, his body trembling with released tension. Lee slid down from his back and hugged his neck, thanking God and thanking her horse. Just then, Pirate scrambled past them, and Slick's head snapped up. Lee held him with the reins, watching his chest, and waited until his respiration had slowed from the pace it'd taken on during the ascent. Then, as Lee stepped into a stirrup, the stallion danced as if he'd just stepped out of his stall after a night's sleep.

Pirate and Juan weren't much more than a dark spot visible only when the rain relented for a moment. Lee put Slick into a splashing lope and peered along with him at the ground ahead. Spotting prairie dog holes was impossible because of the mud and water, but at least she was able to guide Slick away from the larger rocks that were scattered around them.

The dark spot ahead was growing larger. Slick swept past another red trail marker, fighting Lee for his head. She could tell he wanted to launch a full-power assault on Pirate. But she argued him down and demanded he stay at the lope.

Even at that speed, Slick continued to eat the distance between his opponent and himself. Lee could see that Pirate was weaving back and forth. The horse was exhausted, used up, and he was running on heart now— heart and fear of the whip. She leaned forward in the saddle and gave Slick a free head.

Juan must've heard them coming, because he lashed at his mount frantically, quirting Pirate's neck and hindquarters. Slick had pounded up next to Pirate and had started passing him when Lee felt fire across her face and then a sudden, salty taste of blood in her mouth. Juan leaned again to swing at her, and she raised her arm to deflect the blow. The sleeve of her shirt ripped as the whip struck, and a bloody welt appeared on her forearm. For a moment, her eyes met with Juan's.

He raised the whip and swung again. Her hand flashed toward it and locked down at the same moment she tapped her heels against her horse's sides. Slick reacted instantaneously with a surge of speed, and Juan cursed as the loop around his wrist dragged him from his saddle.

Juan sluiced along behind them for several feet, face down in the mud. Then he stood and waved his fist at Lee—and at the rump of Pirate, who'd veered far off to one side and was putting muddy ground between himself and the rider who'd abused him. Lee swung back and followed Pirate for a few moments—there wasn't much reason to hurry now—and saw that the horse was marked on his flanks and muzzle but hadn't suffered severe damage. Carlos or one of her other men would easily be able to get a rope on Pirate the following day, when his panic subsided.

She slowed Slick to a canter and splashed along with him until they were a half mile from Burnt Rock. Then she asked him for speed, and they swept into town at a gallop.

The race was over.

Lee had never been in a saloon before and doubted she ever would be again. But when Carlos had carried Ben's invitation to her and promised her a surprise, she'd agreed.

Even before she approached the batwings, the eye-watering stench of alcohol reached her. She pushed through the doors tentatively, as if she were entering a lion's den.

"Come on in, Lee," Ben called from the back of the room, where he sat at a table with a metal strongbox of money in front of him. "This slop pit is perfectly safe now."

Lee glanced over toward the long bar and noticed there were no bottles resting on it, only shattered glass. A six-inch-wide river of beer flowed from under the bar

188

to the side wall of the saloon, where it was pooling into a sizable lake.

"What in the world happened here?" she asked.

Carlos came in behind her, smiling widely. "My shotgun misfired, an' I thin' some of the bottles may have been . . . well . . . slightly damaged, no?"

Ben laughed. "Funny thing is, it misfired each time Carlos loaded it—nine rounds in all."

"Ees sad," Carlos said. "But what can a man do with a shotgun that don' work?"

Ben stood up behind the table. "It's a strange thing," he said. "My Colt misfired at the same time Carlos's shotgun got silly." He looked around the room. "Doesn't seem like there's a drop of whiskey or beer left in the Drovers' Inn."

"But, Ben . . . you can't . . . wait! Sure you can, and you did! You and Carlos!"

"Wass a terrible accident," Carlos said, shaking his head.

"Awful," Ben agreed. He motioned toward the box of money and the pile of slips with names and numbers on them. "The boys from around here who bet on the race will get their money back, along with some hard words from me. I'm afraid the gamblers and the other scum left as soon as the bottles and barrels started busting. The money they put down will go to the church and to Doc for medical supplies."

Lee nodded. "But what about—"

"Botts ees in jail," Carlos said. "As soon as Ben accused heem of planning Jonas's execution, the rest of hees gang saddled up an' headed out. Murder ees a hanging offense in Texas. They din't wan' no part of stretchin' a rope as . . . how do you say it, Ben?"

189

"Accomplices." He looked at Lee. "I may have given the law a bit of a slant, but nobody stuck around to question it. We even cornered one of Botts's men and got some information out of him before we let him leave town."

"But what about Zach? The clerk at the hotel said he was hurt."

"Zach will be fine. He's at Doc's place now, on a cot. Doc wanted to watch him for a day or so. He's got a doozy of a headache and a smashed nose, but he's a strong man. He'll be on his feet in a couple of days."

A feminine voice startled everyone. "Lee Morgan in a common saloon! I never thought I'd see the day! Next thing, you'll probably dress in men's clothes and ride in a horse race! Shame on you!"

Lee laughed and turned to hug Janice. "I'm sure that'll never happen," she said. "It wouldn't be ladylike."

Janice and Lee moved closer to Ben, arm in arm. "What about that man who rode Pirate, Ben?" Lee asked. "Has he shown up?"

"No, he hasn't. And if he does, he'll wish he hadn't. I doubt we'll see him around here again. Living down being beaten by a lady in a horse race is hard to do in Texas, ma'am."

Janice held Lee's arm a bit tighter. "Carlos told me while you were cleaning up that one of Botts's cronies gave him up to buy himself the freedom to ride out of town. He said that Botts ordered my father's death, and that Juan had been instructed to disable or kill you or Slick—or both. The race was supposed to be a sure thing. Botts couldn't lose—except that he did."

Lee struggled with her voice for a moment. "Yes, he did lose—exactly as he deserved to." She hugged Janice again, then took a step toward the marshall.

"Ben—thanks so very much. I know I've put you through a lot. But I'm sure God will bless you for everything you've done."

He smiled and the dark sacs under his eyes and the tension in his face seemed to disappear. "If he does one day, I'll be real grateful. Right now, though," he said, "I'd sure settle for a hug like you gave Janice."

Lee rushed to him, ignoring Carlos's shrill, teasing whistle and Janice's warm laugh. She'd never been in a saloon before—and she'd never been in love with a lawman before either.

**Paul Bagdon,** a lifelong horseman and former rodeo competitor, reflects his keen understanding of the horse/rider relationship in his writings. Twenty-four of his action-adventure novels have been published in the general market, and he is the author of 250 short stories and articles. Bagdon is currently an instructor for Writer's Digest School and lives in Rochester, New York.